I0587663

ALIEN WAR

LIVE ALIEN CONTACT
BOOK 4

LEAH R CUTTER

KNOTTED ROAD PRESS

Alien War
Live Alien Contact: Book Four
Copyright © 2026 Leah Cutter
All rights reserved
Published by Knotted Road Press
www.KnottedRoadPress.com
ISBN: 978-1-64470-498-1

Cover Art:
ID 35762189 | Spaceship © Philcold | Dreamstime.com Cover and interior design
copyright © 2026 Knotted Road Press

Reviews
It's true. Reviews help me sell more books. If you've enjoyed this story, please
consider leaving a review of it on your favorite site.

Come someplace new...
Do you enjoy exploring strange new worlds, new cultures, new people?

Journey into the various lands envisioned by Leah R Cutter.

Sign up for my newsletter and I'll start you on your travels with a free copy of my
book, *The Island Sampler*.

http://www.LeahCutter.com/newsletter/

Buy More!
Did you know that you can buy directly from the Knotted Road Press website?

https://www.knottedroadpress.com/

ALSO BY LEAH R CUTTER

Science Fiction

Live Alien Contact

Alien Wreck

Alien Codex

Alien Encounter

Alien War

The Long Run

Project Nemesis

Project Nyx

Project Tisiphone

Project Persephone

War of the Allied Worlds

The Complete Labors of Darius Linard

Huli Intergalactic: Science/Space Fantasy

Origins

The Strawberry Girl

Urban/Contemporary Fantasy Series

The Witch's Progress

Circle of Air

Circle of Fire

Circle of Water

Circle of Earth

Seattle Trolls

The Changeling Troll

The Princess Troll

The Fairy-Bridge Troll

The Troll-Demon War

The Troll-Human War

The Troll-Troll War

The Shadow Wars Trilogy

The Raven and the Dancing Tiger

The Guardian Hound

War Among the Crocodiles

The Clockwork Fairy Kingdom

The Clockwork Fairy Kingdom

The Maker, the Teacher, and the Monster

The Dwarven Wars

The Cassie Stories

Poisoned Pearls

Tainted Waters

Spoiled Harvest

Bloodied Ice

The Chronicles of Franklin

Franklin Versus The Popcorn Thief

Franklin Versus The Soul Thief

Franklin Versus The Child Thief

Epic Fantasy Series
The Fallen Elves

ONE

Rosey sighed as she sat in her jail cell and subvocally told Dennis *again* that he didn't need to mount an attack to get them out.

She hoped.

She'd admit that she hadn't been on this side of jail bars for quite some time. (She didn't want to go into the details, given how she'd been released that one time, statute of limitations and whatnot.)

The brig on the Lithic ship was fairly comfortable, at least as far as Rosey's *limited* experience went. She and Jun were together in a caged cell, while Jamaal was by himself, separated from them by a few empty cells. Jun had hypothesized that the Lithic, while they had good eyesight, still possibly relied on their noses more than Humans. Having their other crew members in scent range would be a kindness.

The cell itself had a bunk bed (with Rosey taking the top, of course) and a commode that popped in and out of the wall. That was about it.

Rosey and Jun were currently sitting together on the bottom bunkbed, having a four-way silent conversation between the two Humans, Rosey and Jun, along with the two AIs, Sano and Dennis.

No, you cannot do something foolish like trying to shoot your way out of here, Rosey repeated. *You and I both know that's a suicide mission.*

But what if they never let you go?!?! Dennis wailed.

Rosey just shook her head. Dennis had always been independent, with his own interests, like fashion and interior design. Since when had he grown so worried about her?

I'll be fine, Rosey assured him.

She hoped.

Jun added, *The commanders of the Lithic fleet need to meet to decide what to do with us. Jiac will be able to reason with them.*

Rosey wasn't so sure about that. While Jiac, the Fleet Commander in charge of the three alien squadrons composed of at least thirty ships apiece, as well as the Predator *Nightfall*, had always seemed reasonable, she'd also been incredibly hands-off when it came to the Humans. She'd made Wyrak Hinga, the pack navigator, do all the negotiations between the two species.

Was it a punishment assignment? Jamaal had always thought so. Wyrak wasn't trained to be an ambassador. He was a working stiff, merely a grunt.

However, some of the others on the crew treated Wyrak as if he had a higher rank than he carried, at least as far as Rosey could tell after a week of intense charades while they learned about each other.

Due to the fact that they'd only had a slowly building vocabulary between them, it had been easy for Wyrak to ignore Jun's questions about why the Lithic had appeared with a military fleet.

Who were they at war with?

There had been two clues. One from the Atoylee, an alien race that had been bombed out of existence centuries before.

The other came from the data chips that Rosey had taken off two Lithic warships.

When confronted with the fact that the Humans knew about the Bukoykan, the alien race that they'd guessed the Lithic were at war with, Rosey, Jun, and Jamaal had been thrown in the brig.

Where they'd been stewing for a few hours, now.

Sano piped up. *I've been studying the Lithic computer setup, trying to find a way in,* she admitted. *They have a lot of gapped systems. It's as if they don't trust one system with the next.*

Rosey nodded at that. She didn't know for certain, but she assumed that the Lithic had some sort of bad history with AIs. Everything major computer system on their ships were run by people, not by machines.

Though Human history had a rocky start with AI, by the time the intelligence came to the forefront of the machines, they were well (enough) controlled that no one had to worry about them taking over everything.

So while I could probably open your cage doors, I couldn't necessarily get you any further than out of the immediate area, Sano continued.

Lights, air, navigation, they're all run separately, Dennis grumbled. *So inefficient!*

Rosey rolled her eyes, having already listened to her personal AI complain about the Lithic's lack of imagination when it came to color on their ship.

A guard suddenly appeared, marching down the corridor. The military uniform was loose enough that Rosey couldn't tell if they were male or female. Female Lithic tended to be slightly taller than the males, but you could only see their set of six nipples if the shirt was tight. Otherwise, their features were indistinguishable.

All the Lithic had a lion-like face, with a snout pushed out and eyes larger proportionately than a Human's. They didn't have a mane, but they did have two tufted ears that stuck out on the top of their head and swiveled. The fur that covered them came in a wide variety of colors. Wyrak was tri-colored, being primarily white, brown, and black. This guard was mostly white with black patches around their nose and mouth. Long whiskers stuck out from either side of their snout, and their eyebrow whiskers were also impressively long.

"Jun," the guard said, swinging open the door but not stepping inside.

"Yes, that's me," Jun replied as she slid from the bunkbed and stood.

The guard made the downward motion of their hand that meant *Come here.*

Rosey made to get up off the bed as well.

The guard held their other hand up, palm out.

The meaning of *halt* was obvious, and Rosey wasn't going to push it.

Yet.

"You going to be okay?" she asked Jun as the princess walked toward the cell door.

"Everything will be fine," Jun said serenely.

It kind of amazed Rosey as she watched Jun transform from a goofy, young xenolinguist into a princess of the Emperor's court.

But Rosey had no doubt about who walked out of the area.

Hopefully, it was a good sign that they'd asked for Jun, the recognized negotiator of their group.

"She'll be back," Rosey said out loud, so that Jamaal could hear her.

And she would be.

Or Rosey was going to have to figure out some sort of jail break.

TWO

Though Duri Chung was tempted to instruct her people to fly directly to Ishiman and demand an audience with Emperor Ogawa, she knew that wasn't the way that politics worked. She'd been a part of the Kollective government for too long to make that sort of amateur mistake.

No, it would be better to collect more evidence, including the sale of some of the papers or other artifacts that those grave robbers had found at the Atoylee moonbase.

The xenoaercheologists she'd brought along were grateful enough to be part of the find of the millennium that they agreed to be quiet. At least for now. Duri knew that she only had a small amount of time before one of them rebelled and information about the base was leaked.

They all knew that she was working through channels to do the most damage to the people who'd been at the moonbase first, and that their silence on what they'd found was essential.

Academics understood working the system, even as they bitched about having to do so.

However, as an additional precaution, Duri had sequestered all the brainiacs with the alien materials. It was the only way they could continue to work on the project, code-named Red Elevator (due to the surprisingly bright-red interior of the elevator when they'd forced the doors open).

Duri didn't trust any electronic system, no matter how secure it supposedly was. She herself knew of a number of ways to circumvent such measures. So she didn't give a personal update to General Carrick until they were back on New Rome and she could do so in person.

They met in the general's office, its utilitarian design disturbed by the large screen that the general had unrolled from the ceiling. (It was so ugly and completely ruined the aesthetics. Who had the general pissed off? And did she try to make common cause with them, or side with the general? What would serve her better?) The office didn't contain much else besides the general, his desk, a filing cabinet, and two visitor chairs. Nothing decorated the walls besides a small flag of the Kollective: bright red with the silhouette of a group of planets done in an arc.

Usually, General Carrick sat in stony silence through any presentation that Duri gave. This time, though, not only did he smile, his eyes held wonder at the sight of such a well-preserved alien ruin.

It would have worried Duri if the general hadn't had any reaction: the colors, flowers, and geometric designs on the walls were amazing; the staircase railing with *two* bannisters, the second under the first because the Atoylee had four arms, had changed the scientists' understanding of the aliens; and the obvious living and working spaces of the base brought home how similar they actually were to Humans.

Then Duri got to the part about how someone else had been there. She showed her proof—the obviously Human footprints in the ash and dust, how samples had been taken from some of the key areas—then the most damning piece of all: the empty file cabinet.

When Duri finished, General Carrick sat in silence for a while, processing what he'd just seen.

Duri approved of this. While the general was known as a man

of action, and the medals on his chest proved that, he was also a thinker.

Not as smart as Duri, of course, but so few people were.

"Do we have any proof that it was *those people* at the moon-base first?" the general first asked.

"*Aisha* left Ishiman a little over a week ago, carrying Princess Jun Ogawa, Moe Herath, and Atilio Perez. I cannot find any discussion of where they were going—you know how tight-lipped the servants of Emperor Ogawa are," Duri said. It had always been a sticking point in the ongoing spy game between the Kollective and the Empire. The servants closest to the top people were almost always paid well enough that they never shared inappropriate details about those they served. Leaks were always difficult to find, as well as maintain.

General Carrick merely grunted at that.

"However, the bank that manages the loan for the starship *Aisha* sent a repo ship to the moon Lawaka, and found it there. Despite warnings, the ship fled, and has yet to be seen again," Duri said. "But that isn't all."

She paused for dramatic effect. Damned general merely raised one eyebrow, prompting her to continue.

"There is now a top-level directive from the Empire, delivered to every major supply station, requesting to be informed when *Aisha* makes an appearance. They are warned not to approach the ship, that it is armed and deadly," Duri said with satisfaction.

"So they are in trouble with their own government," the general said, considering. "Do we know who?"

Duri shook her head. "It came through the usual channels."

"I can make some inquires," General Carrick said.

That was intriguing. Who would the general contact? And could she figure out a way to expand her own network to make them a contact of hers as well?

"Good," Duri said. "Just imagine how much more pressure could be applied if *those people* were also charged with robbing a historic alien site. Whatever else is laid at their feet could be disregarded. They might be able to talk their way out of those charges. What they've done on the moon Lawaka is an intergalactic incident and cannot be ignored."

Though Lawaka was officially in the territory managed by the Empire, as it was an alien site, it was considered neutral territory that all governments had access to. Damaging such an incredible could potentially get them into trouble everywhere.

General Carrick nodded at that. "Aye. What about Rosey De Vries?"

Duri kept her face neutral. She'd been deliberately warned away from going after Jamaal Akintola. He'd been a high-level spy for the Empire a few years back.

Rosey, however, was fair game and the general had asked Duri to *handle it*.

"It appears that Rosey was endangering the good people on the space station *Lorenzo*," Duri reported happily. "Her workshop there was confiscated by the station, then sold off to a private investor." The money had come straight from the warlord Constantine, so Duri had no doubts that the price for Rosey to buy it back would be her soul. Possibly with interest.

"Good," the general said. He even gave Duri a smile. "And the xenoarchaeologists are sequestered for now?"

"They are," Duri assured him. Eventually, one of them would crack. The bragging rights alone were just too tempting.

"Keep them under wraps for one more week while I see what I can find out about the search for *Aisha*," he said. "Someone is after them. Perhaps all we have to do is to feed them a little bit more information, so that they'll bring the hammer down even harder."

Duri nodded. That was about as long as she'd assumed this secret could be kept.

The general paused, appearing to be considering his words carefully. "Good work," he finally said. "We're going to get to those people who thought they could fool us. And crush them."

Duri gave him one of the "inscrutable Asian" smiles that she'd perfected over the years. "Of course we are," she said.

Though by *we*, she meant *she*.

Duri was going to find those idiots. With or without the general's help.

And make them pay.

THREE

Atilio sat aboard *The Roadrunner* in the comfortable breakfast nook that Dennis had designed. While his eyes looked out on an unseeable horizon, his hands were busy, stripping apart one of the bigger guns in the rather large collection of armaments that Jamaal had brought with him onto the starship.

He'd worked with this type of gun before. It wasn't standard infantry gear. No, it was reserved for the soldiers he'd always privately referred to as the goons, those who were physically larger and could handle the recoil, but who also were unable to hit the broad side of a shopping mall without a lot of forethought and planning. They couldn't handle the precision of a standard stunner or even a needle laser.

It was an ugly gun, despite its sleek barrel and how balanced the handle felt in his hands.

However, he deemed it to be appropriate.

Atilio wanted to blow a hole through everything he encountered at this point.

The Lithic had thrown Rosey, Jun, and Jamaal into cells.

At least they were still in communication, via Dennis and Sano.

Except that now, they Humans had been separated.

Jun was off talking with the Lithic. Rosey was still in a cell, along with Jamaal, who was evidently in a separate cell.

Harkeen came drifting into the kitchen. He poured coffee into a mug that was probably already half full (Atilio could smell the brandy from where he was sitting, halfway across the room).

When Harkeen glanced over, Atilio nodded, indicating that the tall black man was welcome to join him if he wanted.

Harkeen hesitated, then drifted over to the table, folding himself up as he sat down.

He looked about as lost as Atilio felt.

"They'll let them go," Atilio assured him. Was he lying? He didn't know.

"They better," Harkeen said, giving a ghost of a smile.

The last few hours had seemed to have aged the man years.

Harkeen gave a bitter laugh. "Because if they don't, I'm pretty sure Jamaal will kill everyone who gets too close."

Atilio nodded. He understood better what Jamaal was, the sort of assassinations that the man had committed over the years.

"Hopefully it won't come to that," Atilio said. He finished stripping the gun apart and started putting it back together, his hands automatically beginning the reassembly process without much thought.

"What will you do? If they don't let them go?" Harkeen said.

Why did Harkeen sound so wary? It couldn't be because of the gun, could it?

Atilio knew what he was doing.

"I know that Moe wants to form some sort of boarding party," Atilio said. He shook his head.

Unlike Harkeen and Moe, Atilio had a good idea of exactly what they were facing.

While the Predator *Nightfall* was the largest ship in the fleet they were facing, it wasn't the only Predator class ship out there. Jiac Beowen, as Fleet Commander, was in charge of three squadrons, each with its own Predator. In addition, there were a number of smaller ships that prowled around: Lancers, Maulers, and Darts.

Atilio didn't understand the exact science behind their weaponry. All he could do was count the number of gun tubes he saw on all the various ships.

The total was close to three hundred, and that left him very uneasy.

"A boarding party is suicide," Harkeen said softly.

"Aye," Atilio said, nodding.

The gun had been reassembled. Atilio put it to the side and picked up his own mug. The tea had long grown cold. He grimaced but didn't get up to refresh it.

"I don't know how fast the other ships are," Atilio continued. "I suspect that *The Roadrunner* is faster."

"What are you saying?" Harkeen said.

"A boarding party would be suicide," Atilio said. "But I don't leave people behind," he added with a growl.

Particularly not someone like Rosey.

"Dennis can fly *The Roadrunner* without us," he added. "Because someone needs to know what we've found out here. Before the Lithic decide that we're expendable."

"Do you think they'd do that? Start a second war?" Harkeen said.

Atilio shrugged. "Worst case scenario, yes," he said. "We only suspect that the Bukoykan are the aggressors. We don't know for certain. The Lithic may be the ones trying to expand their territory. Or it might be a civil war."

"That doesn't seem likely," Harkeen said.

"True," Atilio had to admit. "But we don't know. There is *so much* we don't know."

"Except that we don't leave people behind," Harkeen said softly.

"Exactly," Atilio said, reaching for the gun again.

He caught Harkeen's eye, to make sure that everyone knew the page that they were on.

They would rescue Rosey and the others.

Or die trying.

FOUR

Ronald "Ajax" Jackson finally, *finally* got the go-ahead from Constantine to leave Empire space and head back to more familiar stars. He'd negotiated the purchase of Rosey De Vries' workshop. There wasn't anything for him to do there at the space station *Lorenzo* until Rosey showed up again.

Then, he'd come back and bleed Rosey's soul dry.

The other good news was that Constantine had seemed pleased with the work Ajax had done, and the credits had come pouring in. A good captain always shared with his crew, so they were pretty happy as well.

Hell, even Karl "Odysseus" Doukas, his second in command, was starting to look over his shoulder a bit more. A crew that was happy with Ajax meant that it would be much, *much* harder for Odysseus to pull a mutiny.

Ajax had not forgiven Odysseus for holding him at gunpoint on his own ship, *Hermes 3.0*, forcing him to recognize Odysseus officially in the chain of command. It was just a matter of time before Ajax would introduce Odysseus to an airlock.

Probably without a suit.

Ajax found a message from the warlord Constantine waiting for him as soon as they arrived in Allied Worlds' territory.

Was it another bonus for such a well-done job?

Ajax was disappointed to learn that Constantine just wanted them to go harass some ships.

Well, he was a pirate. One of the most badass pirates in the Allied Worlds. Anyone seeing him coming should immediately surrender.

Or suffer his wrath.

Ajax kept Constantine up to date with all his various deeds. Particularly the times he'd had to force ships to hand over crew or goods at gunpoint.

The warlord should be informed of who was willing to pay for his protection and who wasn't. Right?

It appeared that Constantine took care of his people as well. Those who sat under his shield were never to be harassed. Ajax was even directed to attack the scum who'd dared damage one of the suppliers that Constantine considered his.

Ajax understood the protection racket. He'd been working that for years around his home planet.

This was just a much bigger stage. He studied the flow of goods and services in and out of Constantine's empire, looking for weaknesses.

There weren't many. Constantine was scary good. And he had that whole "Greek god" image that worked well on those less sophisticated.

That didn't mean that Ajax wasn't already hatching more plans for how to bring about Constantine's fall. He'd admit that it was going to take more time than he'd originally planned, but he was still certain he could do it.

In the meanwhile, Constantine had sent *Hermes 3.0* out past the farthest reaches of Allied Worlds' space. There were some colonized planets beyond the recognized boundaries that didn't acknowledge any of the intergalactic governments. They were true independents.

At least for now.

Ajax was meeting with some of the locals on the surface of the planet New Orion to see what their needs were. You couldn't just come in and offer to protect a people who had no need of protection. They'd end up resenting what they were paying.

No, there had to be a true threat.

And Ajax knew enough about Constantine's operation that if a threat weren't currently present, one could always be manufactured.

Ajax *hated* being planet side. It was summer in the main city, and the air was sticky and gross. His black leather pants stuck to his skin, chaffing him badly. His bare chest seemed to offend some of the farmers. Too fucking bad for them. His neuro-stimulator ensured that Ajax had the muscles to be impressive, even to these backwater dimwits.

They had the complaints of all farmers: not enough places off-planet to trade their poorly grown and manufactured goods.

If they'd bothered to live someplace that was on an actual trade route, they would have been able to discover profitable crops.

The lovely proverbial farmers' daughters did flirt, and swarmed around Ajax in droves. Unfortunately, none of them managed to make it past the diligence of their fathers, so his bed remained unwarmed.

It was the last night of his stay when a whooping alarm woke him out of a deep sleep. He reached for his gun with one hand and his stretchsuit with the other, before he remembered where he was.

Planet. Free air. He wasn't being boarded. Right.

He stumbled out of the quaint room he'd been staying in, out into the night.

Two large bright stars were streaking through the sky.

Ships?

Fuck. Neither of those were *Hermes 3.0*, were they?

He finally got a comm message through to his ship.

Odysseus informed him that the two ships had just appeared out of hyperspace, exploded, and pieces of them had started falling directly toward the planet. A third was limping toward them, blaring a Mayday on all comm channels.

"What the fuck are you waiting for?" Ajax yelled. "Go and help them!"

Didn't the fool understand that they were there to play the protectors? This was the perfect opportunity! Constantine was going to reward them hugely for bringing this planet under his protection so easily.

"You sure?" Odysseus said. "They're claiming they were attacked."

Ajax paused for a second, closing his eyes and shaking his head. Yes, Odysseus was going to be taking a long walk out an airlock sooner rather than later.

"Yes, I'm sure," Ajax said. "We're supposed to be protecting people. Remember?"

"All right. You're the boss," Odysseus said. "Plotting a rendezvous now."

He cut the comm line.

Ajax stood in the darkness, watching the two streaks of light plummeting toward the ground. Chances were, the crews were already dead. If they weren't, they would be when they met the ground at such velocities.

There wasn't anything anyone could do. As far as Ajax knew, this planet didn't have the equipment to snatch a falling starship out of midair. The best one could hope for was that the debris would land in a large body of water. The next best was that it wouldn't hit a populated sector.

This one was going to be the absolute worst-case scenario: right on top of the main city in this podunk place.

The alarm had been to rouse people, get them evacuated before tons of screaming hot metal landed on their heads.

Ajax fucking *hated* planets.

FIVE

Jun walked calmly toward the conference room with unknown guards surrounding her. Two at the front, two behind, as if she were some sort of dangerous prisoner.

Four wouldn't have been enough to hold Jamaal. Possibly even Rosey, if either of them set their minds to escaping.

For her?

She had no intention of going anywhere but right back to the high command of the Star Pack fleet, to talk, negotiate, and most of all, to *learn*.

Why had the mention of the alien race Bukoykan brought about such a reaction from them?

Jun had assumed that she'd be brought back to the standard conference room that she and the others had spent so much time in over the last week.

She realized quickly that she was being ushered to a different part of the ship, one that she'd never been in.

Lights are different here, Sano informed Jun subvocally. *Softer. Air is better filtered.*

Officer country? Possibly.

The guards stopped. Spread to the sides of an unassuming

door. The one who'd come to get her spoke quietly into a wrist-comm. The door opened.

Jun entered, her head still held high. No matter how nervous she was, she was still a princess, and had been trained to at least always appear serene.

The room was only dimly lit. Shadows hid the walls and corners.

A long table stood at one end. (Or in the middle? It was hard to tell.) Light shone down from the ceiling, highlighting the beings seated in the four chairs: Jiac Beowen and probably the three commanders of the squadrons.

Wyrak was nowhere to be seen.

The little translating device sat squarely in front of Jiac.

While Jun had spent time trying to learn the body language of the Lithic, the lights were such that what little knowledge she had was useless.

She faced an inscrutable board of potentially hostile aliens.

Jiac said something. Only one word was really familiar to Jun.

The translator repeated the sentence in Human common.

"What do you know of the Bukoykan?"

Jun slowly explained what they knew, how she'd first run across the word in the Atoylee papers, then how she'd heard it again in the transmissions from the data chips.

As her eyes grew accustomed to the lighting, she realized that other people were in the room. Possibly that was Wyrak in the corner. As well as Cali, Nysh, and Kalesen, the others who had had the most dealings with the Humans.

"You say that these Atoylee had developed a chemical weapon to use against the Bukoykan?" one of the other leaders at the table asked.

"They were in the process of creating one," Jun corrected. "I don't know how far they got. I do have most of the papers from their facility."

She'd actually stopped reading and looking at the Atoylee papers once they'd discovered the Lithic.

Jiac reached out and turned off the translator as the four commanders started speaking.

Sano let Jun know that two of the Lithic commanders thought she was lying and was actually working for the Bukoykan. The other two, which included Jiac, thought Jun was telling the truth and wanted to work with her and the rest of the Humans.

Finally, the argument between the commanders wound down and Jun inserted herself back into the conversation, speaking the words that Sano prompted her to say in the Lithic language.

"Who are the Bukoykan? Where did they come from?"

It surprised her when Wyrak was the one who stepped forward, turned on the translator, and answered. All of the commanders snarled at him, but none of them stopped him.

What exactly was his position on the ship? He always called himself a pack navigator, third-class. But everyone treated him as something special.

"The Bukoykan are a group species," he started off with. "Not a single mind, like you or me. But a pack that all thinks together."

"Hive mind," Jun said. The concept came from science fiction, not anything that Humanity had actually run across.

The translator gave a word that Wyrak seemed to consider. "Yes," he eventually said. "That's close enough. They don't understand individuals. If you can't be part of their pack they will destroy you. When they first approached us, they showed us many, many peoples that they have already killed."

"Did they kill the Atoylee?" Jun asked. If so, then the Bukoykan were absolutely ancient.

Then a new though occurred. Had they also destroyed the Huzzomi?

"The name of the aliens who attacked the Atoylee is the same. Maybe?" Wyrak shrugged. Then he paused. "And you have never heard of them before."

"That's right," Jun said, nodding. "We didn't know anything about them until recently, and that was only through the Atoylee records."

"Will you join them when they come to you?" Jiac asked.

Jun nearly snorted. "It is almost impossible to get three Humans to agree on what to eat for dinner. Making them all think together? I just don't think that would even be possible."

"They promise peace and prosperity," Wyrak continued. "Across all your people. All your systems and planets. You will be fruitful and prosperous."

"And enslaved," Jun said.

Jiac's whiskers moved upward at that—the Lithic form of a smile.

"That's what we believe as well," Jiac said. "So we fight."

"Would you join us in our war?" one of the other commanders asked.

"How can we?" Jun said, trying to sound absolutely reasonable. "We have never met the Bukoykan. While I believe you, I cannot commit the resources of my government just on your say so."

"They don't negotiate initially, once they discover your kind," one of the others warned. "They will attack, and keep attacking, until you either give in or are destroyed."

Jun shook her head. "Why did we not run into the Bukoykan before now? They must have been in our systems, if they are the same creatures who attacked the Atoylee. Why did they leave?"

Jiac reached out and turned the translator off before anyone could respond.

Sano told her quietly that the Lithic were uncertain. Jun's words made sense to them, but they didn't have an answer. They didn't know enough about their enemy to understand why they'd been in this system, then hadn't stayed to colonize it.

Had they just found traces of the Atoylee, flown in to destroy them, then left again? But no, that didn't make sense. They'd stayed long enough for the Atoylee to fight them. Or at least try.

Or perhaps the Atoylee had originally agreed to be part of the hive mind, only to back out later? Which was why they had so much of the Bukoykan biological workings documented?

The Lithic argument wound down. Wyrak glanced at Jun, then nodded, turning back on the translator.

"You say your people would not join them. What about your thinking machines?" Wyrak said.

More than one of the commanders glared at him for daring to ask such a question.

"We call them AIs," Jun said softly. "Artificial intelligences. They wouldn't really have a say in the matter."

"You are confident in your control of them?" Wyrak pressed.

"We are," Jun said. "We have many horror stories of them taking over. None of those scenarios actually occurred."

"You were lucky," one of the commanders said darkly.

"We were," Jun acknowledged. The rise of the AIs could have gone so much worse than it actually had.

"So how can we move forward?" Jun had to ask. "I would like to think that we would have a common cause, that we could help you in your battles. But we have to know more." She paused, took a breath, then asked, "Will you take us to the Bukoykan? Let us see for ourselves?"

The answer was almost immediate.

"No."

SIX

Jamaal sat silently in his cell. He didn't try to communicate with Rosey and the others. He knew that they'd be in contact with the ships via Dennis and Sano. As he had no such communication channel, he was the only one completely cut off.

No way to reach Harkeen, though he was certain the others were keeping his lover up to date on their situation.

Jamaal had agreed to be present during their negotiations, just in case the Lithic hadn't taken the announcement that the Humans knew about the Bukoykan well.

He had also agreed not to fight his way out of the ship. At least, not initially. He was supposed to let Jun continue to negotiate.

Had that been a fatal mistake on his part? Would the Lithic come to the negotiation table? Or were they all about to be shoved out of an airlock?

The stretchsuits they all wore would protect them in vacuum for a short while. Long enough to be scooped up by *The Roadrunner*.

Hopefully no one was going to try to strip them naked beforehand.

That would make Jamaal fight.

He'd been in tough situations before. Caught in an enemy stronghold with no obvious escape.

He still shuddered when he remembered being trapped in a crawlspace for three days until he finally found a hole in the pattern of the guards and got out.

Though he was in a comfortable cell, and he knew that his friends were still alive and well, this time was far worse.

Harkeen made all the difference.

For the first time, Jamaal was on a mission and had someone to go home to.

Before, he'd always been so alone, living a shallow life. It hadn't mattered as much if he made it to the end of a mission alive. Completing the mission had been satisfaction enough.

Everything had changed, now.

Jamaal ached to see Harkeen again. To hold that strong man in his arms. To hear his quiet chuckle, or to wait while Harkeen gathered his thoughts, sure to say something brilliant.

Jamaal even missed the sludge that Harkeen called coffee, teasing him about the brandy that he occasionally added to it.

Yes, this was the mission of a lifetime. Meeting actual, live aliens. No one would ever be able to take that away from him, that he'd been part of the first crew to do so.

He just had to survive to tell the tale.

And to see Harkeen. Tell him that he loved him. That he'd been a fool to not say so earlier.

To kiss him, one last time.

SEVEN

Dennis was *not* frantic, thank you very much. He was perfectly in control of his emotions. He didn't *do* frantic.

No, he was calm, cool, collected and running through scenarios at the speed of light, spinning up first one situation, then another, then another.

None of them brought him joy.

How was he going to get Rosey out of a jail cell? And really, how careless was it of her to get locked away in the first place?

Then there was the whole getting her out of that alien ship. He hadn't been rude and pinged the ship hard to find her. No, really. He had been doing a lot of very passive scanning, though.

As far as he could tell, Rosey wasn't in the center of the ship, which would have been almost impossible to get to. No, she was on the side, not too far from the airlock and the conference room where she'd been spending most of her time. Seemed to be a direct hallway running from the cells to the door.

How often did the Lithic take prisoners? Were these for the mysterious Bukoykan? Or other Lithic?

The Humans hadn't been allowed to explore the ship. Not that Dennis blamed Rosey and the others for that.

Okay, maybe he blamed them a little. However, he hadn't

pressed the matter. Honestly, who wanted to see that much *beige*? It was a military ship with a completely unimaginative design.

And their computer systems! Maybe, perhaps, he was a little impressed with how paranoid they were. So many of the ship's systems appeared to be air-gapped. It meant a good design, one that was almost impossible for him to take over.

Sano appeared to be just as frustrated. Though it was easier for *her*. She was actually mostly with Jun, contained in that large necklace that the princess wore all of the time. Sano had snippets of herself loaded in other places, and regularly updated herself on what was going on.

Dennis only had *The Roadrunner*.

And Rosey.

When had it become his job to take care of her? This wasn't fair.

Atilio said his name again, trying to get his attention.

"Yes?" Dennis said, bringing his presence to the man.

Of course, Atilio sat in the most comfortable place on the ship, the breakfast nook that Dennis had perfected. Harkeen was with him.

"If we have to break them out, we'll approach *Nightfall* in *Aisha*," Atilio said.

"There are no scenarios where you'll survive such an attempt," Dennis said dryly. Foolish man.

"We know this," Atilio said. "We'll be the distraction, so you'll be able to fly back to known Human space and let the authorities know what we've discovered."

Dennis, for want of a better term, *blinked*. The idea that he'd just go, and let the others die? That wouldn't be right.

"I'm not leaving Rosey behind," Dennis growled. "We're going to get her out of there."

"You're the fastest ship here," Atilio said. "None of the Lithic can keep up with you."

"True," Dennis said, though he wasn't one-hundred-percent

certain. The littlest ships of theirs, called Darts, were supposedly quite fast.

Then again, given how Rosey had tuned his engines, there was a good chance that he was still faster.

"The rest of Humanity must learn about the aliens," Atilio insisted. "And *Aisha* isn't as fast as you are."

Dennis sighed. Out loud for the Humans to hear. "I do not agree with this. I do not agree with leaving Rosey behind. And the others."

"If we have to board *Nightfall*, our mission has failed," Atilio warned. "Getting the information out is the best-case scenario at that point."

Dennis suspected that Atilio might be right.

He didn't like it though. Not one bit.

And while Atilio could ask Dennis to commit to this madness, Rosey was the only one who could *order* him to.

It had better never come to that.

"They're opening the cell door," Rosey suddenly announced.

Dennis conveyed the words to Atilio and Harkeen.

"Are they letting Jamaal out, too?" Harkeen asked, sounding desperate.

"They are," Dennis assured them when he suddenly heard Jamaal speaking from beside Rosey, asking why they were being let go.

"Where's Jun?" Atilio said.

"Don't know," Dennis said.

This waiting! In real time! It was going to drive him nuts. Why couldn't Humans move at computer speeds? Particularly now!

Still, he had to wait with all of them, wait as Rosey and Jamaal were escorted to the airlock, wait as Jun joined them, then wait some more.

"Do we know why they're just being held there?" Atilio asked.

"No, but it sure would be easy to rescue them at this point," Dennis helpfully pointed out. "Wouldn't take any effort at all."

It actually might have been a struggle. One of the Humans would have had to do a spacewalk over to *Nightfall*, then hack the airlock door code, because again, *someone* had built all the airlocks on a separate circuit that neither Dennis or Sano had access to.

So very rude.

Finally, Rosey told Dennis, "We're on our way back. And we have a guest."

"Who?" Dennis asked, but either Rosey couldn't say, or wouldn't.

At least she'd given him a heads-up that they were about to have company!

Was Dennis about to host an *alien*? That had to be a classification far above mere ambassador.

Why hadn't he finished redoing the front airlock and hallway? Not only with the gold crown molding but also the star sequence, so that he could truly be the gateway to the stars?

Time and money, of course.

He sighed to himself and went about ensuring that whoever it was would have the best experience of their lifetime, all the while trying to come up with a title suitable for himself and for such a momentous experience.

EIGHT

Wyrak "Wrong-Way" Hinga was aware that he held a special position in the fleet. He tried not to abuse it. He'd actually been surprised when Jiac, the Star Pack Fleet Commander, nodded to him when he motioned for her to leave the meeting room with him.

"What is it?" Jiac had asked Wyrak as she leaned against the hallway wall. The way her whiskers drooped and her hair was flattened told him just how exhausted she was.

She'd spent the last few hours fighting against the other squadron leaders in an attempt to get the Star Pack fleet, as well as the rest of the Lithic, some help. It looked as though she'd been fighting for days.

And maybe she had been. They had been there for a little over a week now, meeting with the aliens. Only Wyrak had been in direct communication with Jun, Rosey, and the others, but he gave his commander extensive reports every evening.

The negotiations were being recorded, of course. Wyrak tried not to think about that, about how he was messing up.

Wyrak had heard the rumors, of course, about how poorly the war was going for his people. While the propaganda machine tried to make it seem as though the two groups were evenly matched,

Wyrak had not only been in enough battles, but seen his fleets running from them, that he suspected just how badly outnumbered they actually were.

"The other commanders will never agree to show the Bukoykan to the Humans," Wyrak said. "And I agree that they shouldn't be formally introduced," he added quickly when Jiac glared at him. "However, they have to see what we're up against before they'll join us."

"Aye," Jiac said with a sigh. She shook her head then looked at him. "I'm already regretting this. What do you have in mind?"

"Let me go with them," Wyrak said. "I'll go look at the Atoylee base that they've talked about. See the destruction of their home planet. Talk with the Humans about how the Bukoykan have done the same to some of our planets."

Jiac stared hard at him.

Wyrak felt himself swallow down the other words, about how he might, perhaps, *possibly* also be considering taking the Humans and showing them the devastation of the Lithic worlds.

"You know better than to take them into our systems, right?" Jiac said slowly.

"I am aware that I shouldn't," Wyrak said. He was also aware that it could be a potentially deadly move. The Lithic couldn't survive a war on two fronts, with the Bukoykan on one side and the Humans on the other.

However, he wasn't about to swear an oath that he wouldn't take them there.

"The rest of the fleet is going to be unhappy that I'm sending away their 'luck,'" she grumbled.

Wyrak shrugged. "Maybe I can bring us more luck," he said softly.

He was never sure how much to believe the proclamation that he had a third paw, the invisible paw of fate, that frequently touched him, guided him.

It was why he had the nickname Wrong-Way. While he was a good navigator (all right, so maybe only an okay navigator), he did sometimes send the fleet in the wrong direction. However, every time he'd done so they'd actually ended up in the right place.

Like jumping to here, instead of one of the recognized rendezvous spots.

Jiac looked down at the floor. Wyrak could practically hear the arguments going on in her head.

"I'm not officially ordering you to go on what could be a suicide mission," she said slowly. "You are volunteering to desert your post and go with the Humans."

Wyrak gulped. He did *not* want to be known as a deserter. A possible traitor to the rest of his people.

But what else could he do? He knew that he could bring the Humans around, and that with their weapons and technology, the Lithic would have a much better chance at winning their war with the Bukoykan.

"I'm not deserting my post," he said softly. "I just think this is the right way to go."

Jiac snorted at him. "Yeah, Wrong-Way. That's exactly why I'm not ordering you to stay, either."

She paused, her eyes growing hard. "What are you waiting for? Get."

Wyrak froze for a moment, before throwing her a quick salute (left fist brought up to the chest, over the heart on the left side of the body, followed with a quick nod).

Then he was racing through the ship, toward the center of it, heading to his shared room to pack a bag to take with him, needing to quickly figure out everything he should take with him to survive for a month or more.

As he ran, he sent a wristcomm message to Hinx Katmo, to meet him at their room. Hinx was the Star Pack steward and Wyrak's best friend.

Hinx was leaning against the hallway as Wyrak came up. "What trouble have you gotten into now, Wrong-Way?"

Wyrak gave that the eyeroll it deserved as he unlocked the door. While most of the soldiers, and even some of the bridge crew, slept in dorms of twelve bunks per, he'd been assigned a room with only three others. It was a sign of prestige, as at his low rank, he didn't rate that.

"I need nutrition bars," Wyrak said. "Four-week supply. And anything else you think I'll need to survive on an alien starship." The bars were emergency rations, in case a soldier got stuck somewhere. They were fairly bland and Wyrak would be so very tired of eating them after a month's time.

However, neither species had wanted to open up about their entire biology. From what little they had shared, while they might be able to tolerate each other's food, a lot of it was going to cause stomach distress. Or worse.

Hinx's jaw dropped open. It looked kind of funny on him, that pink maw surrounded by all that black fur.

"Where are you going?" Hinx said.

"More moving and getting me nutrition bars, less talking," Wyrak informed him after he grabbed his duffle bag and started stuffing it with clothes from his locker. He only had uniforms, really, no civilian clothes with him. Hopefully the Humans wouldn't mind, even though they were all civilians.

"Okay," Hinx said slowly. He spoke into his wristcomm, placing the necessary order. He also added a couple of boxes of Wyrak's favorite tea, some beer, and some sweets. "Where do you want it delivered to?"

Wyrak paused, holding shoes in one hand and socks in the other.

He'd need extra socks. Would the boots he already had do? Or should he take an extra pair?

"Give me a location, Wrong-Way," Hinx said.

Wyrak gave him the number of the airlock that the Humans would be using to leave the ship.

"I don't like this," Hinx growled. Then he added a set of inhalers to the order.

"I don't either," Wyrak admitted. "However, we have to do something to bring the Humans to our side."

"So the commander is going to sacrifice you?" Hinx steamed.

"She didn't order me to go. She also, very deliberately, didn't order me to *not* go," Wyrak explained.

There were pictures on his wall of his packmates from his first military school, his birth-mother and some of his littermates from home. Beside them was his most recent rank certification, pack navigator, third-class. He stuffed all of them in the bag as well.

"Are you deserting your post?" Hinx said cautiously.

"No," Wyrak said firmly. "I'm going with the Humans on a mission to bring them to our side."

"A mission that no one has assigned to you, that you're taking on your own," Hinx said.

"It's the right way," Wyrak insisted.

At the last minute, he grabbed his slab. It was similar to what the Humans called a tablet, though as far as he understood such things, his had a lot more individual processing capabilities. It also contained some training materials provided by the military about the Bukoykan that he could show the Humans.

Though he wanted to bring more of his things with him, he had everything he needed.

He left the shared quarters. The door shut behind him with a finality that made his hackles rise. Then he strode off toward the airlock with Hinx walking by his side.

"You do know how ironic is it that you're insisting that you're going the right way," Hinx said finally.

"Yes," Wyrak said, sighing.

Was he making a huge mistake? Possibly. Would the invisible paw of fate allow him to do that?

Probably. If it even existed.

Wyrak stopped at the life suit closet and grabbed one, putting it on over his gear.

Hinx held his bag as Wyrak got ready, handing it to him but not letting go, making Wyrak pause and look at his best friend.

"You're coming back a hero," Hinx instructed him. "Or you're not coming back at all."

Wyrak nodded. "That's the gist of it."

As they walked, Hinx explained the inhalers that he'd ordered. While a person could be alone physically, they were rarely if ever completely alone. The Lithic nose always picked up the scents of nearby people.

The inhalers were used by Dart pilots, to give them a shot of scent when they were flying by themselves for too long. It was the easiest way to reassure what Hinx called "the animal mind" that a person wasn't alone and isolated.

"I've given you enough inhalers that you should last for a month, maybe six weeks, if you stretch out the doses," Hinx warned.

"All right," Wyrak said as they approached the hull. "Do you want to come meet them?"

Hinx looked surprised, then nodded.

Wyrak *really* wanted to ask Hinx to go with him. But that wouldn't be fair to his best friend, to ask him to choose between packs.

As they drew closer, Wyrak could see when Hinx scented the aliens and their odd mix of plastics and unfamiliar animal. The chemicals that they used to mask their scents, that sometimes, at least in Rosey's case, just made her personal scent stronger.

Jiac and the other commanders assumed that Jun had some sort of permanent connection to one of their thinking machines —an AI the Humans had called it. So he knew that at least she'd understand his words.

"I'm coming with you," he announced as he joined them.

Jun looked from him, to Hinx, then back again. "Just you?" she asked in the Lithic common language.

He was so going to have to work on her accent! The Humans had initially picked up their language from one of the data recorders they'd found on a Dart ship. The pilot from that ship had what could best be described as a working-stiff accent, broad vowels and a sing-song cadence. It made Jun sound like a country bumpkin and completely unsophisticated.

At least Hinx was polite enough not to snicker, though he suspected an entire new round of gossip about the aliens was about to begin.

"Aye, just me. This is my best friend, Hinx, here to see me off," he added.

"It is an honor to meet you," Jun said smoothly, the words obviously rehearsed.

At least her accent was better with that phrase.

Wyrak turned to Hinx and they clasped forearms, like warriors, before Hinx pulled Wyrak in for a brief hug.

"Hero, remember," Hinx said softly in his ear. "Nothing less."

Wyrak nodded, stepping back. He turned to the Humans.

"Let's go."

NINE

Rosey had *no idea* why Wyrak was accompanying them. Was he going with them to prove to the rest of the Humans that there were live aliens out here? He wasn't an official representative of the Lithic, as far as anyone could tell. Not part of some sort of ambassadorial team.

Or was he being sent because he was expendable?

Once they'd left the *Nightfall*, Jamaal spoke to Rosey on a private channel between their two stretchsuits.

"You need to check for bombs," he said softly. "In Wyrak's bags."

Rosey couldn't help but roll her eyes. "If they wanted us dead, they could have fired on either of the ships and blown us up long ago."

"He might be carrying a biological weapon that could be used against all of humanity," Jamaal insisted.

Rosey sighed. "Fine. I'll ask to search his bags once we get to *The Roadrunner*."

"That might be too late," Jamaal insisted.

"If we're all dead, particularly of something suspicious, Dennis will vent our bodies to space and not allow anyone near until he's one-hundred-percent certain that it's safe," Rosey said.

She was going to have to talk with Dennis about what he'd do when she was gone. She'd offered before to put in some programming that would be triggered by her death which would automatically adjust some of his emotions so that he wouldn't be so devastated that he'd do something drastic.

He'd declined at the time, but maybe it was time to revisit that conversation.

Or to do it anyway...

They arrived at *The Roadrunner* without incident.

As soon as they made it through the airlock, Dennis greeted their visitor in the Lithic language.

Jun snorted. "Seems that Dennis has upgraded himself from *Ambassador of the Court* to *Envoy of the Galaxy*.

"Of course he has," Rosey said dryly. "Could you please ask our guest if we could quickly search his bags? Just to make certain paranoid busybodies happy?"

"Rosey! How rude!" Dennis interjected.

Sano complied with Rosey's request by saying something in Lithic.

Wyrak's whiskers lifted, the equivalent of a smile, as he handed his two bags over to Rosey.

One contained clothes and a few pictures.

The other contained what looked like emergency rations, beverages, and medical inhalers.

"What are these?" she asked, holding them up.

Wyrak explained. Dennis interpreted. "Medical emergency equipment in case he has any issues with our air," he said with a dismissive sniff.

"Satisfied?" Rosey said, glancing over her shoulder at Jamaal.

He sighed, looking as though he wanted to object.

However, the others on the ship came barreling forward at that point, finally allowed into the area by Dennis.

In particular, Harkeen grabbed Jamaal in a great bear hug, actually lifting the other man up and spinning him around.

Moe may have done the same for Jun, while Atilio just gave Rosey a great big smile from the distance.

She caught his eye and nodded. Yeah, she'd been thinking about him as well.

It made *no sense* to get involved with him. He'd be off on *Aisha* soon enough, following along after his captain. Plus, she knew, *knew*, that if she let him get any closer, he'd get under her skin. Larry, the chemist back on *Lorenzo*, was a casual thing.

Atilio was too intense, too focused, too *good* for just a fling.

Fortunately, before she did anything foolish like go and hug the man, Dennis spoke up again.

He spoke in Lithic then in Human common, pummeling Wyrak with questions about what he liked, what sort of routine would he like to follow on the ship, and what could Dennis do to make his stay more comfortable?

Wyrak looked a little dazed, to be honest.

Rosey snorted and caught Wyrak's eye. She picked up one of his bags, handed him the other, then made the hand gesture that the Lithic did which meant, "Follow me," before she walked down one of the corridors.

Wyrak followed along, warily answering Dennis's questions with practically a monotone.

It took Rosey a few moments to process what was happening.

"Dennis," she said softly. "Let me ask the questions. You can just interpret. Okay?"

"But that's so inefficient!" Dennis complained immediately.

"I know," Rosey said. She wasn't about to explain to him that Wyrak wasn't thrilled about talking with an AI. Not until she had some time. "Please do it anyway. You want your guest to be comfortable, don't you?"

"Fine," Dennis said with an expressive sigh.

Was her ship getting more emo? Hopefully not. He was enough of a handful as it was.

So Rosey fell back to walk beside Wyrak, explaining the ship's décor as they walked from airlock that was slightly utilitarian, along the first corridor that had a desertscape painted on the walls, with a cartoon coyote off in the distance, a nod to the ship's name. At the next junction, they entered a jungle hallway that was lush and green, a refreshing step away from the starkness of the desert. The third hall—that contained all the guest rooms—had beautiful mountains and vistas.

"Who did all of this?" Wyrak asked as he looked around at the various wall.

"Dennis did," Rosey said. "He is the thinking machine that runs this ship."

"Huh," was Wyrak's response.

"Not what you were expecting?" Rosey guessed.

"No, not really," he said. "The thinking machines, in the past when they had more free rein, disdained all art, considered it unnecessary."

"Our first AIs were trained on art," Rosey said. "They have a deep appreciation for it."

"Interesting," Wyrak said.

"You'll be here," Dennis said as a door to the left slid open.

Rosey walked in first, knowing that Wyrak would be more comfortable if she did.

The Roadrunner had six guest rooms: three suites large enough for two people, as well as three single rooms. Mostly, they sat empty. However, Rosey sometimes traveled with a crew of pilots on their way to a race, or with a committee of people from Racing Oversight. (Then there was that one time Jamaal had talked her into carrying all the guests for his birthday party. While it had been fun, even Rosey had found herself wincing at the amount of sparkles and debris that had been left behind, to say nothing of having to listen to Dennis's complaints. She still found glitter in odd corners occasionally.)

Dennis had put Wyrak in one of the suites, large enough to accommodate two people, such as the room that Harkeen and Jamaal were in. Atilio, Moe, and Jun all stayed over on *Aisha* most of the time, though Dennis did have single rooms set up for each of them as well, in case they needed to rest while they were visiting.

Rosey showed Wyrak the facilities, as she suspected that they'd be slightly different than what the Lithic used. (She'd never been to a restroom on the Lithic ship. The stretchsuit came with that plumbing already attached, and it was just more convenient to use that rather than to try and slide out of it, then back in again.)

"Would you like a tour of the rest of the ship?" Rosey asked, putting his bag down.

Wyrak nodded, then tugged at the suit he wore and said something.

"He'd like a few minutes to freshen up," Dennis said. "Jun needs to give the tour. You need to get up front, boss."

"Jun will be here to guide you," Rosey said, leaving the room in a dignified manner, then hoofing it up to the helm, assuming that Dennis would tell the princess of her tour guide duties.

The Lithic ships were all sliding away. She watched them pull back, then one-by-one, they turned and vanished.

Without a word of goodbye.

Well, crap. That wasn't a good sign.

She really wanted to understand their technology better. A Human ship needed to reach a certain velocity before it could dive into hyperspace. The Lithic ships were barely moving before they just dropped away.

Was that to do with their shielding? Their engines? While Wyrak knew some things, he wasn't an engineer. He couldn't tell her about the physics his people had discovered.

Rosey sat back in her captain's chair and sighed.

She'd give Wyrak some time to settle in. Maybe not even worry about him much until after they'd all gotten a good night's sleep. If she could wait that long. Which honestly? She wouldn't bet on.

Then, they were going to have some long conversations about what they should do, where they were going next.

And why exactly was she carting this alien around.

TEN

Moe hadn't allowed himself to consider what might happen if the Lithic hadn't let Jun and the others go.

He knew that he, himself, would have done anything to get Jun back. Even go on a suicide mission.

While he would have preferred waiting those few hours on *Aisha*, he'd gone over to *The Roadrunner* when he'd learned that Sano was still in communication with Dennis.

The AI had never been invited into the computer system on *Aisha*. She'd complained that there wasn't enough space for her there.

Maybe he was going to have to focus on updating the computer systems next, so that the AI would have a vacation spot, as it were.

Particularly now that the disrupter guns would no longer blow them up. It might make sense to have an AI on board, who could react to a hostile threat more quickly than a Human.

Then again, Moe wasn't certain that he wanted to cede that much authority to an AI. Atilio certainly wouldn't approve.

However, if it made Jun more comfortable, he'd do it.

Moe had already met Wyrak, though the navigator hadn't been Moe's primary contact. Instead, he'd been working with

Merssin, the fleet steward, to talk about what the Lithic carried, what the Humans carried, and what sorts of supplies they might have in common, that could easily be provided.

Trade made the galaxy go round, at least as far as Moe was concerned.

If he could become the primary transportation company of Human goods to the Lithic...his fortune was assured.

Maybe, *perhaps*, if he acquired such a position, he'd have moved up enough social ranks that his pursuit of Jun wasn't complete folly.

It gave him hope. Even when the Lithic had grabbed Jun and the others. Even when the fleet disappeared, leaving only Wyrak behind.

Moe had always been told that he was lucky. He'd been born the seventh son of a seven son. Even carried all seven names around with him as a reminder.

Sometimes the weight dragged him down, but today, despite everything, he felt uplifted by that background and those traditions.

Particularly as he walked with Jun, giving Wyrak a tour of *The Roadrunner*.

They were all in agreement that showing him the engines was one step too far.

They did walk around everywhere else. Moe hadn't been to all the places that Jun led them to. Not because he'd been forbidden, but because he'd never asked. Wyrak seemed particularly enamored with Rosey's exercise space, and Jun assured him that he could come and use it at any time.

Wyrak had many questions about the empty holds, where Rosey carried the speedships that she built. That devolved into a long conversation about racing, which put a speculative look in Wyrak's eyes.

Seemed the Lithic didn't have such a sport. Their contests were always held planet-side. They did have a lot of athletic sports and could be very competitive.

Yet another opportunity for cultural exchange! And profit.

After a quick consultation with Dennis and Rosey, they also showed Wyrak the alien wreck that they carried, one of the Lithic Darts.

They'd never admitted to having it, and seeing it was an obvious shock to Wyrak.

He asked some sharp questions about where it had been found, when, and in what sort of condition.

Jun was able to reassure him that no body had been with the ship and that though they'd scanned the area, they'd never found a pilot.

Wyrak only seemed partially mollified.

Moe understood.

"We would have told you immediately, when you showed up, if we'd found a body," he assured Wyrak.

Bad enough that there were things that he didn't feel comfortable telling an alien. He still didn't want to be *that guy*.

While *The Roadrunner* was big enough to contain an aeroponics room for fresh food, Rosey didn't have one. Instead, she had a top-of-the-line food printer. She also had some shelf-stable foods and a small freezer. However, given the amount of time that they'd spent out in space, plus the number of mouths that she was feeding, she was running low on just about everything. *Aisha* was actually slightly better off, but that was because Moe had stocked up before they'd left, so he could be ready to travel for weeks without making a stop.

Wyrak seemed familiar with the concept of a food printer, though he'd never used one himself. As Rosey didn't have scanning capabilities, it wouldn't be able to recreate anything that Wyrak had brought. He didn't seem to be that excited about only eating the nutrition bars of his, then again, while the two species had some similarities in terms of biology, they'd never done a deep dive to figure out what each other could eat and what would kill them. They'd only done enough to know that they could share some of the basics, like water, tea, and coffee.

Still, Wyrak went back to his cabin, then rejoined them in the kitchen nook, getting some hot water for the tea he preferred. Dennis had proclaimed it similar to coffee given its stimulating property. However, it would also be an acquired taste for a Human.

They shared stories of their growing up. Wyrak seemed fascinated that Moe had so many brothers and sisters (ten total, a reasonably sized family on his home planet). Wyrak had had two families, as far as Moe understood. One was his birth family, or pack, that had consisted of him and three girls. A birth-mother would generally only have one litter in her lifetime, though occasionally would have two. They lived together as a family would.

Then there was his milk-mother, the one who he stayed with part of the time, with kits who weren't part of his birth pack. Moe would equate her to a wise old aunt, like his own Aunt Deepa. In olden times, the milk-mother would have also provided supplemental nutrition to the kits. In the modern day, when nutritional supplements were readily available, she was just a guiding figure.

It seemed that most of the elders who Wyrak looked up to were female. Not that the Lithic was a maternal society, but they had leanings that way, more so than many of the Human cultures that Moe was familiar with.

Moe left the table to go cook with Harkeen, providing a hand when it came to spicing everything perfectly. The food smelled wonderful, even though nothing was fresh.

Dinner was a crowded affair, and they dragged in a second table. Dennis complained that they were ruining the aesthetics of the entire room. Wyrak only took a few mouthfuls of the dishes that smelled good to him, not wanting to get sick accidentally. He ignored most of the vegetables and stuck primarily to the proteins.

They all retired to the recreation room after dinner, each with their favorite beverage. Moe was surprised that Jamaal and Harkeen were still there. He assumed that they'd want to retire early that night, to get reacquainted with each other.

Though he didn't have that sort of relationship with Jun, he did sort of wish that they could do the same.

He needed to have patience, though. There were too many hurdles still in the way before he could further pursue his suit of her.

Rosey brought everyone's attention to her by standing up. She raised her glass of red wine and toasted to all of them for surviving an encounter with aliens. Next, she proposed a toast to Wyrak and welcomed him to the ship.

Then the atmosphere grew serious as Rosey stared at Wyrak.

"Now, while I don't usually work as a taxi service, I'm happy to do so at this point. Problem is, I don't know why you're here or where you're going. Care to enlighten us?"

Wyrak looked uncomfortable, but he nodded, stood, and began speaking.

ELEVEN

Ajax paused the recording of the incident, then replayed the last thirty seconds of it again.

What in all the names of the Gods of Hades were those little balls?

The ship that had escaped and survived had managed to record a few minutes of the surprise attack on their planet before turning tail and running.

The two ships that had been with it had turned at the same time. They'd all been shot at as they'd entered hyperspace. Sheer luck was the only reason any of the three ships had survived the transit.

However, popping back out into real space had been too much stress on already damaged equipment, and two of the three ships had literally torn themselves to pieces. Only the largest chunks had survived entry into the atmosphere. About half the main city on New Orion had been decimated by the falling shrapnel.

The stuck-up mayors and other politicians were now all looking to Ajax for a fucking handout. Too bad he had nothing to give them.

Hermes 3.0 wasn't large enough to carry a second starship

with it. There was no way for him to get a message back to Constantine, not without physically traveling to the closest system himself and finding a transmitter.

So while Ajax played the would-be rescuer of the entire system, and stayed on the utterly gross planet, he'd sent Odysseus back with a message. *Hermes 3.0* could do the roundtrip journey in about a day. Then it would probably take another couple days for the news to get to Constantine, and for him to send a message back.

And yes, while Ajax was nervous about sending Odysseus anywhere on *Hermes 3.0* without him, Odysseus voluntarily gave his word that he'd come back as quickly as he could. He'd even said it in front of members of the crew.

Sure, Odysseus would double-cross Ajax at some point. Probably not now, though.

In the meanwhile, Ajax went over the recordings that the surviving ship, *Eyes On You*, had made.

There was no up or down in space. Sure, some idiots thought that toward a planet, any planet, was down. They were wrong. One of the things that Ajax had learned from Rosey was that while a speedracing course was linear, the best pilots thought outside of that.

Eyes On You had been on an elliptical orbit, as far as Ajax could tell. The planet the ship had been orbiting, Jazawa, shone brightly in the bottom left corner of the recording.

A dark beast of a ship filled almost the entire right side of the screen. Little balls vomited forth from its belly.

Even at extreme magnification, Ajax had difficulty determining what exactly those little balls were. Eventually, he'd concluded that each one of them was an individual ship, blasting absolutely everything in its path.

A single little ball couldn't do much damage.

This large of a swarm of them could probably take down even a Kollective Defender.

Fuck.

Were they alien? Or some other Human government that had drawn a line in the sand, saying only this far and no further? There were always stories about other Human colonies that had been formed far outside the reaches of known space.

While Ajax would bet on it being Humans, he'd seen too many strange things recently to bet against the aliens.

From the short recording that Ajax had, he could see them shooting down every ship that was in orbit around Jazawa.

Then what? Would they enter the atmosphere? *Eyes On You* hadn't stuck around to see what other damage those things could do, if they were capable of bombing a planet from outside the atmosphere.

Ajax's first inclination was to board *Hermes 3.0* as soon as it returned and get the hell out of there. He was *not* curious in the least to take a closer look at whatever had happened.

The captain from *Eyes On You*—a curvy black woman who still appeared to be shell-shocked—had also brought news that a couple of the other colonies out further had gone dark. No one had heard from them in a while.

It could be that there'd been a problem on the colony itself. That sort of thing happened. People who left the safety net of regular trade routes didn't always make it.

Or perhaps something like this stupid huge-ass ship had shown up there as well, dropped its load of little ball ships, and destroyed everything.

Odysseus actually brought *Hermes 3.0* back into orbit around New Orion after delivering his message.

Good boy. Ajax wasn't going to have to kill him. Not yet, at any rate.

The next three days, Ajax spent time traveling from New Orion to *Hermes 3.0* to *Eyes On You* and back again, meeting with people who thought they were important, never making any promises but using all the empty, weasel words that he could to calm people down without ever actually saying anything. (Fortunately, his parents, and in particular, his father, gave him a good model to follow when it came to that.)

Finally, Ajax felt that enough time had passed and that *Hermes 3.0* should go back and check on the inner system, see if there were any messages from Constantine.

He wasn't about to send Odysseus on his own this time. No, if he was lucky, Constantine would look at the situation, declare it hopeless, and wash his hands of it.

So Ajax made more empty promises about returning as soon as he possibly could before he hightailed it out of there, back toward inhabited space and civilization.

He'd been expecting messages as soon as they hit the inner system.

He hadn't expected to be hailed by other ships as he approached.

And not just one ship.

No, Constantine's entire fucking fleet.

"Welcome, Ajax, far flung traveler!" Constantine's soothing baritone came over the comm as soon as they were in hailing distance. "Let us meet and discuss our new, glorious future together!"

Crap.

Ajax couldn't shake the bad feeling he had about all of this.

He couldn't just disappear though. Constantine's reach was too long.

Ajax had no option but to comply.

And hopefully he'd survive whatever madness this faux Greek god was about to unleash.

TWELVE

Jamaal had kind of hoped that Rosey would manage to acquire some patience and not ask Wyrak about his intentions until the morning. He really wanted to spend some more time with Harkeen in their suite. What they'd managed this afternoon had been fun, but they hadn't had enough time.

Nowhere *near* enough time.

Then again, would a lifetime be enough? Jamaal was no longer certain.

Wyrak stood up and started to speak slowly, a few sentences at a time, so that Sano could translate.

"Do you know my nickname?" he asked.

It seemed that none of them did.

"I'm called Wrong-Way," he explained.

Rosey snorted. "Funny name for a navigator."

Wyrak's whiskers lifted. "Proving it wrong was part of why I applied for navigation school in the first place."

That made Jamaal smile and nod. He'd always liked the young alien. That he was that contrary made him even more relatable.

Wyrak explained how he'd first gotten the nickname, how he'd gone the wrong way along a race course and had ended up saving an older woman's life.

"She proclaimed that I had a third paw, an invisible paw of fate, that pressed down on me now and again," Wyrak finished up.

He paused and looked at each member gathered there before he continued. "When I go the wrong way, it generally turns out to be the right way," he said after a few moments.

It had seemed to Jamaal that the Lithic were more superstitious than some. Humans came in all extremes, of course. But as a society, it had felt to him that the Lithic took their superstitions seriously.

Jun spoke up. "So while your rank is pack navigator, third-class, the crew consider you something more, yes?"

"Yes." Wyrak shook his head. "Some of them consider me their 'luck.'"

Jamaal interrupted before Jun could sidetrack them down a long cultural discussion.

"Are you here to bring us luck?" he asked.

"I don't think I bring anybody luck," Wyrak said. "I just...go where I need to. Even if my destination was originally someplace else."

He told them about how the fleet had found them, how after the battle they'd been in, he'd been the one giving the instructions to meet up at one of the regular rendezvous sites.

And how they'd ended up there instead.

"The engineers *still* can't figure out how I managed to program that particular jump into the system. It shouldn't have been possible," Wyrak said. "But what do engineers know?"

Jamaal kept his snort to himself seeing Rosey and Atilio bristle at the remark.

"So what is the right way, Wrong-Way?" Jamaal asked.

The navigator grew a little more solemn and stiff.

"I would see the destruction that was wrought by the Bukoykan on the Atoylee," he said softly. "I would see this remarkable moonbase that you've described." He took a deep breath and sighed it out. "Then, maybe, I will show you some of the destruction that the Bukoykan has wrought on our systems, on our planets."

He paused, then shot them all a hard look. "I will not introduce you to the Bukoykan. That is the wrong way. But I will show you them. Then, you will have to make up your own minds, whether you will help us. Or not."

Wyrak sat back down.

Though the young navigator tried to be stoic about it, Jamaal could see the fine tremors in his arms, the general uncertainty of his being.

"Thank you, Wyrak," Rosey said. "You have given us much to think about. As it's late, and we've all had an extremely eventful day, I suggest that we go get a good sleep. Tomorrow, the Humans will meet and decide what we're going to do."

Wyrak stood. "Thank you." He gave them the Lithic salute, a fist bumped against the right side of their chest and a short nod, before he strode from the room.

"Well? What do you think?" Jamaal had to ask.

Rosey just rolled her eyes at him. "I think that I'm going to sleep and make my decision when I'm awake and more fresh in the morning."

"I concur," Jun said. "Wyrak has given us a lot to think about, and I'm not about to jump the wrong way, as it were."

She got up and left the room, followed by Moe and Atilio. Rosey trailed after them.

Jamaal turned to Harkeen.

"What about you?" he asked as Harkeen reached out and took his hand. Goosebumps ran up his arm, originating where Harkeen gently rubbed his thumb across Jamaal's wrist.

"I think we should do as Wyrak asked," Harkeen said softly. "Show him the Atoylee. See the destroyed worlds in his systems, and whatever else he'll show us of the Bukoykan. All the while, preparing reports of what we've seen so we can send them at a moment's notice."

That got Jamaal to smile. Yes, they needed to see more. And

while Jamaal was by nature more paranoid than anyone else present (with the possible exception of Atilio) he was also inclined to side with the Lithic in this war.

"Now, what am I going to have to do to make sure you sleep tonight?" Harkeen asked as he stood, pulling Jamaal up with him and into a hug, holding him close.

"Oh, I don't know," Jamaal said. "I'm pretty worked up already about the aliens and all."

That got a deep, sexy chuckle that he felt as much as heard.

"Oh, I know," Harkeen said. "I think I have just the cure, though."

Jamaal couldn't help but grin. The *look* that Harkeen shot him set his heart racing.

However, before he could allow himself to be seduced, he had one more thing to do. He paused where they were, arms wrapped around each other.

"You know I love you, right?" he said. It was the first time he'd said the words, but they felt *right*.

"I do," Harkeen said solemnly. "And I love you as well, more than I can say. But..."

"But what?" Jamaal had to ask when Harkeen didn't continue. What strings was his lover about to insist on?

"Maybe I can show you," Harkeen said with a kiss that did nothing to calm Jamaal down.

They happily made their way back to the suite that Rosey had provided to them and eventually, Jamaal actually did get some sleep.

THIRTEEN

As Duri had predicted, the secrecy around the Atoylee moonbase lasted about a week longer.

Then again, she was the one who'd provided the leaked information.

There might have been an *angry* tone to the piece, blaming the state of the site on those grave-robbers who'd arrived at the location before proper scientists could secure it. Possibly even a note about how poorly run the location was. The planet Zonami, in the Kollective territory, where the Huzzomi aliens had been discovered, at least had a satellite circling it to record all traffic going to and from the system. (That was a lie, but one that the general public would easily swallow, given that it was something that the Kollective would do. And possibly should do, now that Duri was thinking about it.) But Niani had no such satellites, no such protections. Shame on the Empire for not taking that initiative to protect this valuable site!

She had to admit that the buzzing from the wasp's nest that she'd kicked amused her greatly. She spent the morning reading through the various news articles on her tablet while sipping the excellent tea provided by her assistant Kiley.

Finally, though, it was time to get back to the rest of her work.

Primarily, finding the other aliens that Duri was certain were out there. Of secondary concern was tracking down Rosey *et al* and seeing to it that they suffered greatly.

Were those aliens the Bukoykan? The same as the ones that the Atoylee papers mentioned?

Of course, it concerned Duri that the Atoylee appeared to have been at war with the Bukoykan. That had always been a Human fear: that the aliens Duri so desperately wanted to meet were aggressive and insistent on domination, not negotiation.

It was one of the reasons why she approved of the Kollective's military might. General Carrick had other uses, she supposed. Certainly his budget did.

However, were the Bukoykan the same aliens as the ones that had built the alien ship that Duri had so briefly had in her possession? The manufacturers of the data chip and so on?

It would mean that their civilization was ancient. Given what she'd seen—the metals that the ship had been manufactured out of, the data chip—it didn't feel to her as though those belonged to a race that had been around that long. The technology was possibly a step or two beyond what Humans currently had. But nothing so far outside their realm as to appear magical.

No, she would bet that the race who'd made that alien ship wasn't the same as the Bukoykan, that the latter were long extinct.

Too bad. She would have liked to meet aliens whose prowess and might would be a test for the Kollective.

Assuming, of course, that Humanity would win whatever war they waged.

Just as Duri was starting to delve into her other reports, General Carrick issued a request for her presence in his office.

Duri chose to think of it as a request, and not as the thinly veiled demand that it was.

Had the general already figured out that she'd been behind the leak?

Oopsie.

Duri walked into the general's office with the most

"inscrutable Asian" look she could manage. At least the offensive screen had been put away, rolled up and disguised on the ceiling. The office was empty and stark, matching the general's stoic silence as she walked in.

"Sit," General Carrick ordered after letting her stand for a few moments too long as he stared at her.

What? Did he think that the junior varsity glare he'd been giving her would cause her to sweat? He didn't know her well enough if he honestly believed that. (And she had an aunt or two who could teach him a lesson.)

Duri sat with her usual grace and calm. While she was certain that the visitor's chair she sat in measured heart rate and other biometrics, she had nothing to fear from such examination.

"What did I tell you about not going after Jamaal Akintola?" the general fumed.

Duri didn't have to affect the surprise that overtook her. "I haven't gone after him," she said. "I have left him completely alone, as you requested."

The general just grunted. "Then what was that clumsy attempt at the space station *Lorenzo* to get him arrested?"

"It wasn't me," Duri snorted. "If I'd issued that, it would have gone more smoothly." Or so she assumed.

The ploy from the Racing Oversight that she'd run hadn't gone according to plan, but the general didn't need to know the details of that.

"It was an obviously false warrant," the general complained.

"And it didn't come from my office," Duri assured him. "I didn't issue it."

"Then who did?" General Carrick seemed greatly confused.

"I don't know," Duri said, shrugging. "You told me not to investigate him, to stay hands-off. So I have."

She knew about the warrant, had learned about it sometime before. Was the general just getting up to speed on what had happened? Why had his reporting network failed him?

And how could she break it further?

"Now, if I believe you, and I'm not completely certain that I do, who would do such a thing?" the general asked. "What other players are on the board?"

Duri didn't roll her eyes, no matter how much she might want to at this point.

Did this general actually expect her to fill in all the gaps for him?

"I'm aware that someone bribed the bank that owned the note on *Aisha* to get them to call it in based on non-payment. And that the Empire now has an official notification warning about that ship," the general ticked off. "Are the player or players who put those into play one and the same?"

Duri didn't want to give the general any more information than he already had. However, she did know more. Was he just testing to see how much she'd tell him? She'd assumed that her team was already reporting on her.

Could it be that they were slightly loyal to her and weren't telling him everything? Was he actually this clueless? Or was this all a test?

Duri had to make a decision about which way to jump, and though she normally abhorred "going with her gut" at this moment, she had no other choice.

"The warlord Constantine was the one who bribed the bank," Duri said.

Given the slight nod that the general gave her, she assumed that he'd already known that.

"However, he didn't do that on his own. He was prompted to by someone else. Someone with deep enough pockets to pay him to do the bribe. Someone from the Empire," Duri said. "I don't know who," she added. *Yet.*

"And the notice about picking up *Aisha* had to come from someone highly placed in the Empire," the general mused.

"Exactly," Duri said. "I do *not* know for certain. But I would guess that that order, as well as the order to detain Jamaal Akintola, came from the same person."

The general nodded. He seemed to be considering for a moment, before he pulled a single folder off a short pile on one side of his desk and slid it across to her.

"The warlord Constantine called together a massive amount of ships, gathered them at the edge of Allied Worlds' space where they waited together for a few days, before taking off," he said, nodding at the folder.

Duri opened it and found the report that the general was referring to.

"He wouldn't need that large of a fleet to take on *Aisha* or *The Roadrunner*," Duri said immediately.

"I know that." General Carrick actually seemed amused by her comment. "I don't have a spy who's close to Constantine. My source can only report on movements, not reasons."

Duri nodded, impressed by the general's reach.

"So what do we do about it?" she asked. She wasn't sure where he was going with all of this.

"There's an alien species that's closing in on Human space," the general announced. "I've sent Defenders to the far reaches of the Allied Worlds' territories. I don't know where Constantine has gone, but I'm assuming that it's to meet these aliens."

Duri barely managed to contain her shudder. That would be one of the worst case scenarios that she could imagine. This pimped up "Greek god" being their first contact! It would give the aliens a completely incorrect picture of Humanity.

"What I need you to do is to focus on finding Rosey De Vries, Jamaal, and *The Roadrunner*," he continued. "At all costs. They're the ones who have been closest to finding the aliens. They've disappeared for the last few weeks. Have they made first contact? Or were they blown up in the process?"

"I'll find them," Duri said with much more confidence than she felt.

One of the first things she needed to do was to replace the team that was on Lawaka. After the scientists had determined that they couldn't stabilize the moonbase, that it was a hopeless cause and that all they could do would be to record the disintegration, they'd set up remote cameras and left the vicinity.

Duri would send a new ship back, until she could prod the Empire into putting up permanent surveillance in the area.

Rosey and the others would return to the scene of the crime.

And she'd be waiting for them.

FOURTEEN

It didn't surprise Atilio that, come morning, the unanimous vote was to continue as Wyrak had suggested, first going to Niani to see the Atoylee world and possibly the moonbase, then to visit one of the destroyed planets in his system. Wyrak let them know that taking them there would go against the Lithic military position, but he would be willing to do it anyway.

Besides, it was going to take some time to figure out the navigation. While Wyrak was a navigator, the Lithic star systems here were all unknown to the Humans, including the one that the Lithic had popped out into.

That wasn't the first concern, though.

They really needed to resupply.

Aisha couldn't approach any of the usual space stations they used for provisions. There was too much of a chance that the bank that owned the note for the starship might have put out a general notification about them and that they'd be retained.

Fortunately, Dennis could send out their order ahead of their arrival at a space station, then make sure the flitter only had to pause long enough to pick up everything. (While bitching the entire time about how he *needed* to be attached to a station, at least for a little while, in order to get started on his next interior design project.)

The next question, though, was whose credits were they going to use?

All of Rosey's assets had been frozen, probably illegally, due to shenanigans on the space station *Lorenzo*. While Jamaal had accounts that weren't strictly linked to him but to one of his personas, he didn't trust that his cover hadn't been blown.

Moe didn't have access to the kind of credits that they needed. Neither did Atilio.

No one was going to touch Jun's credits. Those would be tagged immediately by whatever watchdogs had been put in place.

Harkeen turned out to have enough, but just barely. Jamaal had consoled him that morning by saying that if they weren't all arrested at the next port, when the news broke about the Lithic, he could make a killing selling stories about his life and the alien encounter. That had brought snickers from everyone.

They'd popped out of hyperspace into an area controlled by Allied Worlds. It was the closest system to where they'd been, also one of the least populated. The space station *Dionysus 5* dealt in as many black-market goods as regularly traded items.

Unfortunately, due to some convoluted rules (or perhaps, as this was their first time there and they didn't know who to bribe) no one would load an unmanned flitter. Someone had to fly the ship to the station so they could physically sign for everything they picked up.

Which was why Atilio found himself in the helm of said flitter, flying toward the space station.

There'd been some argument about who should go. No one would risk Rosey. Jun was adamant that Moe couldn't go. The only other person qualified to fly the flitter was Atilio. (Jamaal had claimed that he could do it, but he really couldn't prove it, particularly after the pop quiz that Dennis insisted on before allowing *anyone* near his equipment.)

Wyrak had seemed amused by all the various machinations. He'd been curious about the flitter, though he understood that there was no question that he'd be allowed to fly it.

Atilio hadn't spent as much time with the alien as the others. However, he felt just as convinced that they were following the "right way" as directed by Wrong-Way.

The thought may have made him giggle to himself more than once.

Atilio was *not* impressed as he drew up to the space station *Dionysus 5*. At least half the lights on the space station to make it visible were either burned out or dim. It was long and skinny with fifteen small disks circling the center core, each one being its own deck and probably with its own special clientele. Something had recently struck the decks toward the bottom, probably space debris or an asteroid. Normally, shields should have protected the station. Were they broken? Or too expensive to be maintained? The damage had yet to be cleared, and he didn't see any workers scurrying around in space, either.

Where would the most shady deals be made? At the top, where it was the easiest to attach and leave the space station? Or on one of the lower decks? Possibly that spot to his left as he approached, the place where it was dimmest?

He was directed to land the flitter on deck five, so about one third of the way down the stack. He was fine with that. They weren't *important people* after all.

He just wanted to get in, get loaded, and get gone.

The area Atilio pulled into was obviously for loading and unloading cargo. Mostly empty berths stretched out on either side of the flitter.

Atilio stepped out in his stretchsuit, without the helmet up, and immediately regretted it. *Someone* needed to replace the air filters in here. The rank air, full of funk from too many people gone too long without even using a sonic cleaner, pressed down on him.

Jamaal had given a credit stick to Atilio just before he'd left *The Roadrunner*, full of untraceable credits. Atilio was incredibly happy to have it, as the first thing he'd had to do was to bribe the floor manager to get his goods loaded.

He could see the pallets sitting *right there*. But the floor manager was going to take his own sweet time getting Atilio's supplies loaded. The manager had even suggested that Atilio needed to go find some "entertainment" while he waited.

Atilio just shook his head, certain that the floor manager was going to get a kickback from whatever place he visited.

The bribe seemed to work, though, and it only took two hours for the job to be finished (instead of the twenty minutes that an *efficient* space station would take).

Atilio was tempted to put up his helmet while he waited, but that would just be rude. Plus, he didn't want to stand out.

Just a regular working stiff, like all the rest of y'all.

Fortunately, trouble didn't rear its ugly head until after he was on his way back to *The Roadrunner*.

Unfortunately, trouble did show up.

"You're being followed," Dennis told Atilio just after he'd pulled away from the station.

"Are you sure?" Atilio said. While his own paranoia was pretty high, who would follow him?

"Affirmative," came Rosey's voice over the comm. "Two transports." She suddenly swore. "They have guns. And possibly an electro-magnetic wave field."

Atilio was a sitting duck. No, worse. A *waddling* duck. Flitters didn't have the speed that a transport ship did.

"I need you to dive. Now," Rosey commanded.

Atilio obeyed, feeling for a moment like he was back in the military.

The little unnamed flitter responded immediately. When he pressed on the yoke, it also started noticeably accelerating.

Of course. Atilio should have realized that any ship that Rosey owned had engines faster than what the original specs said.

"Yup. They're following," Rosey said, sounding grim. "Turn twenty-five degrees to your left. Dive again, hold the position for one minute, then come up sharply."

Atilio did so, not certain what Rosey was doing. Was she testing the capabilities of the other ships? Checking his own speed and reflexes? Or just maneuvering him out of the way?

Possibly some combination of all of those.

"Good," Rosey said. "Now, level out, and turn another sixty-five degrees to your left, keeping up your acceleration."

Atilio smoothly turned the flitter and continued to hold down the yoke, surprised that he was still gaining speed.

Damn. He was going to have to bribe Rosey to work on the flitters that *Aisha* held.

"Have you been hailed yet?" Rosey asked after a few moments.

"Nope," Atilio said, double checking the comm. "Not a peep."

"They're still right on your tail," Dennis grumbled. "How rude."

"All right, I need you to slow down and dither for a few moments," Rosey said. "Make them think that you're winging all of this."

"Okay," Atilio said slowly. He wasn't exactly sure how to do that, but he tried. First, he pulled to his left, then his right, zigzagging for a bit, before trying the up and down thing again.

The station was still a brightish spot to his left. He was closer to it than he had been. He couldn't see *The Roadrunner* anywhere.

"Okay, now you're going to play chicken," Rosey said after a few more minutes of silence. "I want you to run directly at the other ships."

A chill cast itself across Atilio's shoulders. "All right," he said quietly.

He wasn't sure why Rosey thought that sacrificing himself and the little flitter was the right move, but he was going to do as she asked, hopefully so that the rest of them could get away cleanly.

"It was good knowing you," he added as he turned the flitter, preparing his soul for whatever came next.

"What?" Rosey came back immediately. "Oh, no. You're not getting away from me that easily. No, you're going to run at them, dive when I tell you to, then pull back, hard, flying up from behind them and over the top of them while upside down."

"Oh," Atilio said. He had no idea that a flitter had that sort of flying capabilities.

Then again, Rosey's ship.

Finally, Atilio faced his foes. They were two brutish looking ships, bristling with gun tubes.

Atilio didn't give them a chance to react. He pushed down on the yoke *hard*, accelerating faster than he thought he could.

A couple wild shots came at him, but nothing even close enough to ding him.

He could already hear Dennis's complaints if he damaged one of *his* flitters.

"Dive!" Rosey said loudly.

Atilio did exactly as she said, going down rapidly, flying below the ships, then pulling back up behind them, flying over the top of them at speed, then continuing to wing himself away.

The Roadrunner suddenly loomed in the distance.

"Coming in hot," he warned as he aimed for the open ship-hold.

Civilians didn't have dampening fields to catch runaway ships. Not like the military.

Correction.

The *majority* of civilian ships didn't have dampening fields.

The Roadrunner did. So while Atilio still slammed into the hold hard, the damage was significantly less than it could have been.

He sat panting in his seat. His shoulders and chest were going to be bruised from where the harness had caught him.

But he was there. Alive. With their supplies.

And maybe, perhaps, with a bit more interest from Rosey than he'd originally thought.

FIFTEEN

Mornings were always the worst for Wyrak. The air was too stale (or too fresh, depending on your perspective). No comforting scents of other Lithic nearby.

He'd considered asking the thinking machine that ran *The Roadrunner*, Dennis, to maybe turn down the filtering of the air in his room, just so that he could at least smell himself in the morning.

He'd decided not to. One, because that might be even worse, to only be able to scent himself. And two, it was a weakness that he didn't want to admit to.

So every morning, as soon as he woke, Wyrak took a small puff on one of the inhalers that Hinx had provided. He didn't want to think about how uncomfortable he'd be without them.

Possibly even crazier than he already was.

At first, he'd used the inhalers several times a day. Now, he strictly limited his intake to once in the morning, intent on making the supply last.

The comforting smells of home filled his senses. If he closed his eyes and took another deep breath, he could almost imagine himself back on *Nightfall*.

However, as much as Wyrak might want to believe in some invisible hand of fate, he was also a realist.

He opened his eyes and stared up at the alien ceiling.

Such a small thing. The color. But it was all wrong.

Did the Humans see a different spectrum? There hadn't been any scientists aboard the fleet ships. However, the medical doctors had speculated that was the case based on the colors of the Human clothing.

The white was just too bright. He missed the comforting gray of the Lithic ships, the warm browns and beiges.

Whereas Dennis was all about color.

"Good morning, Dennis," Wyrak said. It still made him a little uncomfortable, talking with a thinking machine. But Dennis had never acted like the ones from the Lithic past.

Mostly.

The machine did consider himself to be as important as any of the real people onboard. However, he wasn't vying for command. He'd complained about them not stopping at that space station, but that was just so he could do more changes to the interior design of *The Roadrunner*. Not so that he could take over.

"Good morning, Wyrak," Dennis said, speaking in Lithic common.

At least Wyrak had been able to correct the thinking machine's accent. It amused him that sometimes Jun still sounded like an old soldier who'd grown up on the wrong side of the space-port, with too many littermates and not enough credits.

The sound of another's voice also brought Wyrak some peace, a touch of the comfort of home, in this alien place.

"Should I let Jun know that you're awake?" Dennis asked.

"Yes, please," Wyrak said. That was another thing that had surprised him. The Lithic never ate alone. Being forced to have meals unaccompanied was a punishment. Humans thought it was normal.

Then again, they had single births with only the occasional

twins. Just twins were rare in a Lithic family. Mothers usually gave birth to multiple mouths. In ancient times, many of the littlest kits died young because they were so much smaller than the rest of their birth pack. Even the milk-mothers might not be able to make up the difference. Very large families had also been the norm. Now, in modern times, Lithic mothers only had one birth pack. Occasionally they might have two, but that was a lot of mouths to feed, as well as care for.

Wyrak liked the sonic cleaner that the Humans had. It left his fur silky and fluffy, which had surprised him. He took a few moments to grind down his claws, keeping them at a polite length.

Before he left, Wyrak touched the pictures he'd put up on the wall next to the door: his birth-mother, his littermates, and his pack mates from college.

Every day, he reminded himself why he was doing this. For them. So that their planets would be safe from the destruction issued by the Bukoykan.

He just gave a smirk to his navigation certificate.

Was he going the right way? The wrong way?

Only time would tell.

Wyrak was always impressed with how hard Jun studied his language, how much mastery she'd gained in it.

Then again, this was her field of study. Xenolinguistics.

They were able to hold a fairly in-depth conversation in Lithic common that morning over breakfast, talking about the foods that had meant the most to them as children. And her accent was slowly improving.

There were a lot of terms that neither of them could translate, as the ingredients were indigenous to each species and had no equivalent.

It was still a very good exercise for Jun, and an excellent way to build vocabulary, trying to describe various tastes. They'd even started up one of the tablets so that she could show him pictures of what she was talking about and he could help her figure out the correct descriptive terms.

After they'd finished with the "lesson" as it were, they both fetched themselves some more tea. While Jun's smelled good, it tasted awful. She felt the same about his.

They sat for a few moments in comfortable silence, just enjoying the morning, the tea, and each other's company.

However, Jun started talking again. Wyrak had noticed this about Humans. They were so much more chatty than the Lithic. Any sort of mates could spend more than an hour just sitting in silence. Longer if the other people were part of a pack. The Humans that he'd run into so far didn't appear to have that ability.

Jun had shown him recordings of the monkey species that Humans supposedly descended from. They, too, were never still. No such equivalent remained from the Lithic home world, which had been lost in the war with the thinking machines. He'd also seen recordings of the great wild cats, the lions and tigers, as well as the domesticated breeds. The species that the Lithic had descended from and were genetically close to had survived. The Human cats and the Lithic's ancestors did share a vague resemblance.

"We'll be reaching Niani later this morning," she said. "The Atoylee home world."

She spoke in the Human common tongue now. Seemed that it was his turn to struggle finding words.

Wyrak wasn't sure whether it would be appropriate to ask, but decided that he had to know anyway.

"Will anyone be there, again, to chase us?" he said. He'd been aware of the wild flight that Atilio had had to make to get away from the space station where they'd resupplied.

"I don't know," Jun said with a sigh.

Wyrak wasn't as good as some of the popular characters from fiction, who supposedly could always scent when someone spoke the truth. However, he was getting much better at discerning Human emotions.

Jun was both telling the truth, that she didn't know, as well as feeling frustrated with said truth.

"But that's why we're going to Niani first," she admitted. "If someone else is in the area, they're much more likely to be orbiting Lawaka. So we're going to time our approach to come in on the opposite side of the planet, away from the moon."

Wyrak nodded, assuming that he'd gotten the gist of what she'd said, even if he hadn't understood every single word.

"Plus, there are the *razzure* storms," she added.

"The what?" Wyrak asked. It was a word he didn't know.

Jun repeated the word. *Razor.*

"What does that mean?" Wyrak asked.

Jun found a picture on the tablet to show him. "Both men and women sometimes use razors to keep some of the hair off their skin. Like on their faces. However, we can also use a cream that removes the hair for much longer periods of time."

They talked about the blade, how sharp it was.

Wyrak kept his shudder to himself.

Removing fur wasn't something the Lithic did voluntarily.

Then Jun showed him pictures of Humans who hadn't removed their facial fur.

Wyrak hadn't realized that was a possibility. He had just thought the Humans were mostly hairless.

They got back to the topic of the *razor* storms, how they'd gotten that name due to how the winds shredded everything in their path.

Wyrak nodded. The planets that the Bukoykan had destroyed hadn't developed such winds, but he suspected it was a possibility. Most of the planets had burned for a couple of years and had only recently grown cool enough to visit.

Terrible massacres. Terrible waste.

They spent more time chatting, Jun telling stories about the digs she'd been on, admitting to actually funding a lot of the research.

It had taken some time to find the equivalent of a princess in Lithic. It wasn't a current form of Lithic government. They'd moved to a Council of Worlds with the attack of the Bukoykan. Before, there had been a loose alliances of planets with no one regulatory body over everyone.

That the Humans only had three major governing bodies had surprised him. They occupied a large area of space as far as Wyrak understood the star maps that Dennis had shared with him.

However, they had a much smaller number of planets than the Lithic. Only three hundred to their five hundred. And their population was much smaller as well. Humans liked space. Lithic tended toward density.

Dennis announced that they were about to reach normal space, so everyone should hang on.

Wyrak grabbed hold of the table in the breakfast nook, just in case.

Jun merely smiled at him, sat back, and took a sip of her tea.

Was Dennis joking about the transition?

Wyrak nodded when they reached real space, and took a deep breath, releasing the tension in his lungs. While Humans could *see* the changes that hyperspace wrought, the black lines that evidently marked every edge, the Lithic were more in tune with how the scents changed. Everything smelled off, as if their nostrils were plugged with something floral. The smell was different every trip, as well as for each person, so scientists had never figured out a way to block it. The Lithic could see a bit of what the Humans did, the lines and such, but it wasn't as sharp for them.

This confirmed for him that the two species really saw different light spectrums.

"No ship in the vicinity," Dennis announced. "No trackers on this side of the planet."

Jun gave him a smile. "Ready to go walk on an alien world?"

Wyrak nodded.

Was he ready? No.

But this was the right way to go about bringing the Humans to their side in the war.

He just knew it.

SIXTEEN

Rosey flew the flitter down to Niani, carrying Wyrak and Jun. Though Atilio had said that he'd be fine flying the ship and following her instructions if there were a problem, Rosey wanted to do it herself. She was the best pilot they had.

Plus, she wanted to step on a planet that had once held aliens. She hadn't gone down into the moonbase, unlike the others. She'd only seen the pictures.

Jun was also insistent on going. She'd be the translator for Wyrak, as well as their guide, since she had the most experience on Niani.

They landed well away from any of the dig sites. The entire planet had been mapped out, and the various teams had only done archaeological work in areas that ground-penetrating radar had predicted would give them the best returns.

They also had to consider the razor storms. This was the "off" season on the planet for digs, as this was the time when most of the storms occurred. There were a few in the distance—one to the north and two to the west. However, they were at least a day away, so the surface should be safe. For a while.

Rosey didn't mind planets, unlike some of the other space-farers she knew. Sure, there was *weather* to deal with, along with such inconveniences as night and day, the lights being automatically dimmed instead of when she wanted them to be.

However, she also considered each planet a *challenge*.

How could she set up a race here? What sorts of parameters would there be? What would she need to modify on any flier she built?

Niani, she had to admit, would be tough. Though Jun had assured her that during the time when the storms weren't ravaging the planet, shrubs grew; currently, it looked pretty flat and uninteresting. Pretty much all Rosey could see was a light, brownish dirt. And more dirt. And still more.

Dennis was already giving her a hard time about the amount of *dust* that would clog the flitter she'd brought down to the planet.

"What drew people to this planet in the first place?" Rosey had to ask Jun. She would have thought that the first survey team that ran across this place would take one look at the planet and jump to another system, despite the fact that there was an atmosphere and breathable air.

Sano translated her words to Wyrak before Jun replied. "I'll admit, it isn't much to look at. However, the upper atmosphere carries residue of strange chemicals, things that don't occur naturally. That got people curious enough to actually land here." She paused as Sano translated more. "There was one person, Teodoro Khuu, who was instrumental in getting the world properly mapped and explored. They were the person who brought in the ground-penetrating scanners. In their notes, they constantly said that they could feel that something more was here."

Jun shook her head. "Teodoro was obsessed with Niani and the Atoylee. Even though they knew that a razor storm was coming, they didn't leave when they should have. They died here, and the last of their finds were destroyed."

Rosey nodded, unsurprised. It took a special type of person to go digging for alien remains, to hold the faith that they'd find something in the face of all obstacles.

One might even say obsessive.

"This happened because of the Bukoykan?" Wyrak asked in passable common.

"Yes, we think so," Jun said, nodding.

Wyrak gazed out over the horizon.

Was that a bleak look in his eyes? Or was Rosey just assigning that to him? She, herself, felt pretty bleak thinking about it. While she lived on a space station, and the Kollective assholes were in charge of Earth, she still wouldn't like for a similar fate to occur there.

Jun talked more about what used to be on Niani. The inhabited parts were mostly semi-tropical, filled with trees and animal life. The Atoylee were less of a manufacturing race and more of a chemically based one. There were theories about how the Atoylee created a range of chemicals and how each individual worked with their environment. So their buildings were organic and made out of trees and other natural things, rather than built out of stone and steel.

"There is nothing here," Wyrak said. "How do you know?"

"There are a couple of things that support this theory," Jun said. "One, we found children's books buried far underground, the type that explain the world to young ones. That find also contained a grammar and spelling book. We were lucky to have found those, and learned much about the Atoylee as a result."

She took a deep breath before she continued. "We have come across a second alien planet that was destroyed in wars. The Huzzomi. Their remains are completely different. You can find piles of melted metal and stone on the surface. Though they were destroyed just as thoroughly as the Atoylee, their ruins contain more things for us to find."

"The Bukoykan meld together organic with metal," Wyrak said. "They grow their ships. Like a clusters of eggs, all together."

Rosey just nodded and kept her surprise to herself. Wyrak hadn't talked at all about the Bukoykan or what the Lithic knew of the other species.

Wyrak curled one lip in a snarl. "And if one ship loses contact with the other ships, it will blow itself up."

Oh. That must have been a rather nasty surprise for any of the Lithic who'd captured one of the ships to study.

They walked around a bit more, but honestly, there just wasn't much to see. No ruins to build on. No pictures to draw inspiration from.

Just a desert of dirt, with practically no life remaining.

They were on their way back up to the ship when Dennis gave the warning that another ship had entered the system.

A Kollective transport.

And it was heading straight for them.

"Hang on!" Rosey called back to the others.

The shielding in the flitter wasn't good enough to survive hyperspace. However, it was much better than what one would normally find in such a ship.

The engines were also much faster.

So Rosey pushed them hard and fast through the atmosphere, not worrying about frying anything as she ascended. They made it back to space in record time.

"Do not tell me that you're coming in hot," Dennis warned as Rosey approached.

"You know I am," Rosey said.

"But I haven't finished fixing the docking bay from the *last* time someone damaged one of my flitters by coming in too fast!" Dennis complained.

"We'll get *The Roadrunner* back into top-notch shape as soon as we can dock at a space station again and not be worried about getting arrested," Rosey said, trying to soothe him.

That merely got her a snort, followed by a sigh.

"You're too old to be indulging in all this juvenile delinquency," Dennis said.

Rosey rolled her eyes. "I'm not that old," she told him as she centered the flitter's nose on the opening of *The Roadrunner*.

There wasn't any more time for commentary as they *slammed* into the hold.

"Ow," Rosey said, her shoulders already aching from where the harness had kept her in her seat. "Dennis, get us out of here."

"Already gone, boss," was the unsurprising reply.

"Everyone okay back there?" Rosey said as she unhitched herself, turning around to look at Jun and Wyrak.

Jun's pale face and wide eyes merely stared at her before she gave the slightest nod.

Wyrak appeared to be glaring, dividing the look between her and Jun.

"Why are you hiding from these new people?" he asked. "Are you *brzzta*?"

Sano helpfully supplied the translation of the word Rosey hadn't understood.

Criminals.

"No," Rosey said. "Not really. Look. It's complicated," she finally ended up with.

Wyrak merely shook his head and undid his harness, then stalked out of the flitter muttering to himself.

Rosey wasn't sure what all the alien was saying, but she knew that he had to be questioning whether he was actually going the wrong way or not.

SEVENTEEN

Ajax should have known that Constantine's personal transport would be about as gaudy and decadent as they came.

Most of the other ships the warlord had gathered together were bigger and bristling with guns. He'd even found something that looked like a Kollective Defender. (Ajax learned later that it was an older model Defender that had been decommissioned, yet somehow hadn't made it to the junkyard to be stripped, and all the useful parts recycled.)

Constantine's ship was more like a yacht, designed to look sleek and fly faster than the rest. Plus, despite its size, it was capable of going through hyperspace.

Ajax stepped through the airlock into a Greek garden, complete with ivy growing up the walls and a sparkling, splashing fountain in the middle of the vestibule. Or whatever the hell you'd call the small room he found himself in.

Giggling girls came up to him, all dressed in traditional Greek togas. The cloth covering their tits was whisper-thin, as were their gauzy skirts. They insisted on stripping him of his stretchsuit, getting all the way naked, then dressing him in a similar toga, though at least the cloth was white and substantial.

He understood why. Stripping him made sure that he wasn't

carrying any weapons with him, not unless he'd hidden a gun someplace very uncomfortable. And he was certain that some doorway scanner would have already alerted security if he had been.

Was Constantine that paranoid about being attacked by his own people?

Possibly.

"Ah, Ajax! My worthy emissary! Come, bring me news!" Constantine's voice commanded from one of the overhead speakers, like a god issuing commands from the heavens.

"Right away," Ajax said, dipping his head, responding automatically.

A part of him screamed that he was being manipulated, while the rest of him kept quiet about it.

He had to play the part if he was going to survive this madhouse.

The girls led Ajax through hallways painted with murals that made it look as though he were traveling along a road in the Grecian countryside, with hills in the distance sometimes giving way to sparkling blue waters. The air smelled sweeter than usual ship air, probably tinted with some floral essence. Carpet softened his footsteps, making it feel as though he walked on clouds. Despite the warmth in the ship, he still shivered.

Everything here was designed to seduce the senses.

He started doing math in his head, trying to cling to rationality at any cost.

Constantine was holding court, as it were, in an area designed for lounging. Simple music played, acoustic flute, drum, and tambourine. Perfumed air made Ajax's head swim. Beautiful mosaics covered the floor. The walls had projections on them, windows overlooking more Greek countryside, providing bright spots around an otherwise dimly lit room. Another fountain splashed in the corner.

Couches circled an open space where a young woman performed, dancing sensually while picking grapes from one tray, then the next, eating each lasciviously. Three men were there with the warlord, rough looking men who appeared as uncomfortable in their togas as Ajax did. However, they all appeared mesmerized by the woman, or possibly dazed by Constantine himself.

"Good, good!" Constantine said as Ajax approached. He clapped his hands and the music halted abruptly. The woman popped the grape she'd been licking directly into her mouth and gave the warlord a grin and a wink.

"Thank you, Aphrodite, for that lovely performance," Constantine said. "You shall be rewarded immensely. Please wait in my cabin."

"Of course," Aphrodite said, licking her lips. "I look forward to serving you. And any others you desire."

With a flounce, she sashayed her way out of the collection of couches.

Constantine actually had to clear his throat to bring the other men's attention back to him.

At least he looked bemused and not pissed that all eyes hadn't been focused on him the entire time.

"Brave, gallant Ajax! Herald to new worlds! What wonders you have brought to my attention!" Constantine said grandly. "These are my generals," he continued, introducing each to Ajax.

They all had pretentious Greek names: Damocles, Leonidas, and Menelaus. Ajax treated them with respect because until he knew where they stood, it would be stupid not to.

Constantine waved one hand at one of the projections on the wall. The pleasant window disappeared and the recording of the attack took its place.

The generals finally shook off whatever had been holding them lethargic as they stood and walked over to the projection.

"What in the name of Hades are those?" Leonidas said.

"Those represent an opportunity," Constantine informed them. "I came here to see what sort of protection I could provide to this community of planets. Fortunately for me, I didn't have to manufacture anything! Look at those savages!"

The three generals glanced at each other before looking back at Constantine.

"That's a pretty massive attack, sir," Damocles said.

"They were attacking an unarmed planet," Constantine said with a dismissive wave of his hand. "They could have been disrupted with a strong enough force. Or possibly made to think twice before attacking, given the size of our fleet."

"So what are you planning?" Menelaus asked, still staring at the attack that was running on a loop.

Yes. That was the point exactly.

What *was* Constantine going to do about this entire situation?

"Now, gentlemen, I know it should not surprise you that I've been in contact with others who swear that there have been aliens traveling among our stars," Constantine said. "Living aliens."

Ajax just nodded. He'd been the one who'd told Constantine about Oswald, and stealing back the actual alien parts from him. He'd also shared the pictures he'd taken of the data chip and the little reader that Oswald had created.

Had Constantine found Oswald in his lair? Made him an offer he couldn't refuse?

Ajax would bet that even Constantine had to walk carefully around the computer hacker extraordinaire. Or he might find his fountains hijacked and himself constantly being splashed, or some other mischief.

The generals, though, were much more skeptical.

"Really?" Menelaus said. He stepped forward, as if by some prior agreement, he was to be their main focal point. Probably lost a bet to end up in such a horrible position, the short end of the stick as it were.

"I will make such data available to you, back on your ships," Constantine said dismissively.

Menelaus glanced back at the other two. They all appeared to be in agreement.

"Why do you think this attack is from aliens?" Damocles asked, his attention going back to the recording.

Constantine gave an exasperated sigh. "I do wish you could keep up with me," he said.

Ajax didn't roll his eyes as much as he wanted to. He'd heard variations of this complaint before, how Constantine was so much *better* and *faster* and *smarter* than the average Human, and what a shame it was that no one else could accompany him in his brilliance!

Then again, if anyone could, they'd probably be seen as too much of a threat and would end up taking a naked walk out of an airlock.

Constantine waved his hand again and the recording change. It zeroed in on just one of the ships. Calculations of size, speed, potential damage by its guns, estimates of shielding, and every other measurement that could be guesstimated flowed on the edges of the frozen image.

Then the recording focused in further on what little could be seen of the pilot of the little craft, fuzziness being washed away again and again as they drew closer.

The image could easily inspire nightmares.

That wasn't a Human face.

The creature appeared to have wide eyes at the top of its head. Some part of Ajax's brain whispered that it was possibly a compound eye. Instead of a nose, it had a flat area that went down to two mandibles. Underneath that was some sort of mask, probably providing oxygen or whatever the hell that thing breathed. Though its arms were covered in a suit, they still seemed thin and jointed wrong. And there were too many of them.

As one, the generals recoiled back.

"What...what the fuck?" Leonidas said.

"That, my dear gentlemen, is our enemy," Constantine purred. "And we are going to save the galaxy from them."

The generals glanced at each other.

Ajax could practically hear the commentary. *Yeah, right.*

"I've assembled a large enough fleet to completely wipe out the attackers recorded here," Constantine told them. "We have more than enough firepower amongst us." He took a deep breath, then said, "*Trust me.*"

The amplified words echoed and repeated throughout the room, striking Ajax solidly in his breastbone. He stopped himself from automatically bowing in the face of such majesty, but just barely.

The generals responded immediately, like they'd been trained (or conditioned) to. They started falling all over themselves to assure the warlord that they did trust him. Of course they should trust him. Constantine knew what he was doing. He'd studied those recordings, gamed out all the alternatives. They would be victorious!

Laughing and congratulating each other on the victory sure to come, Constantine accompanied the generals out of the room and to the airlock, sending them back to their various ships.

Only after the warlord had left did Ajax find himself shaking off whatever "spell" Constantine had put over him.

That image of the alien pilot still stared coldly at him from the recording.

Ajax shivered.

Constantine was certain that he'd win. He'd convinced his generals, probably through constant conditioning, that if they trusted him, all would be well.

The depth of coldness that still crept along Ajax's spine promised him otherwise.

EIGHTEEN

Jun stared out of the front screen of the flitter as they flew across the still-smoking remains of what had once been a bustling planet. Wyrak had insisted that they come here first, see the destruction, before he'd show them the recording of the attack.

The devastation was so immense Jun couldn't wrap her head around it.

She was aware of some of the military operations that the Emperor engaged in. Sure, there was occasional damage in those. Possibly parts of a city would be bombed. (There was always reparation after such an occurrence, or so the PR machine of the Empire assured her).

Nothing on this scale.

Emperor Ogawa had never ordered a *planet* destroyed. That she was certain of.

Rosey flew them. She appeared to be swearing under her breath. Jamaal had insisted on coming with them. He, too, was stunned.

Dennis had already made recordings of the planet from space. Of course, he'd complained about potential damage to *another* flitter.

However, they had to see it for themselves. Up close.

Wyrak had insisted on it.

After they flew back to *The Roadrunner,* a glum group gathered in the recreation room that had been adapted as their conference area, with a couple of tables pushed together and some chairs.

Jun had heard Dennis apologizing to Wyrak about the aesthetics of the place more than once.

Wyrak held up his slab. It surprised Jun that he'd evidently already worked out an interface with Dennis, because he was able to plug it in immediately, and what he had on his little screen now appeared on one of the walls of the room.

"This is the Bukoykan," Wyrak announced.

Jun tried not to recoil automatically. She only partially succeeded.

Moe and Harkeen grew very pale, while Atilio and Rosey sat stoically.

Jamaal was the only one who actually leaned forward to get a better look.

The being on the screen had two large black eyes set on either side of their skinny head. Those took up most of its face. A short, flat bone-white part went down from there, before splitting into two large, sharp-looking mandibles. Underneath those was a gaping mouth.

It had four rather skinny arms that had multiple joints. The hands each ended with what looked like a set of two pinchers. The arms came out of a barrel-shaped torso, that was in turn supported by two thick, stumpy legs.

"Insectoid?" Jamaal asked.

"As far as we can tell, yes," Wyrak said.

Jamaal nodded to himself. "No shoulders. Very little upper body strength. Strong legs, though."

Of course, Jamaal would be thinking about how to fight such a creature.

"You said they were a hive mind," Jun said before Jamaal

started asking about pressure points and where a killing strike should be directed.

"Yes," Wyrak said. "They told us about that, once they stopped bombing planets. Like this one."

"Wait, so they destroyed worlds before talking to you?" Jun asked, confused about this point.

"Aye," Wyrak said. He shook his head. "They claim that they tried to communicate, but that no one responded. So they assumed we weren't intelligent."

"How do they communicate?" Jamaal asked, also looking confused.

"They use sounds that aren't in our hearing spectrum," Wyrak told them. "They also have a chemical language. However, there's a lot of skepticism that their initial attacks were 'accidents.'"

"But you were able to communicate? Find common ground?" Jun asked. While she might be initially repulsed by the sight of the Bukoykan, she would hope that she'd be able to overcome that and treat them like intelligent beings.

Someday.

"Sort of," Wyrak said. "They offered to bring the Lithic into their galactic empire. They could *convert* us so that we'd be part of the hive mind. Some sort of genetic engineering."

The group practically shuddered as one at that.

"Of course, some did consider that an option, spouting off that it would bring galactic peace to our people."

Though Jun didn't see Wyrak give that an eyeroll, she suspected that was due to some level of discipline on his part.

"We were introduced to at least two other races who'd joined the hive mind of the Bukoykan. They seemed...lifeless. So in the end, as a people, we decided that wasn't our path."

Wyrak was quiet for a moment after that, as if deep in memories.

"What happened?" Jun asked quietly, drawing the young person back from whatever they'd been remembering.

"They attacked again," Wyrak said bleakly. "Destroyed another world. If we wouldn't join them, we would all be killed."

"That's aggressive," Jamaal said dryly.

"Tell me about it," Wyrak said. "That was four years ago. We've been fighting a losing battle ever since." He waved his hand. "Sure, the high command tells us that we're evenly matched, and it's just a matter of time before we overwhelm them. I've been in too many battles. Seen too many attacks. We are *not* evenly matched. We're just barely holding on."

He sighed and looked down, obviously deeply troubled by the war and what he was saying.

"We need help," he said softly.

He shook his head, then reached for his slab.

The insectoid being was replaced with a recording of an attack.

Atilio swore softly as they watched three large, black ships vomit out hundreds of small, ball-like ships above a planet.

"Attacking the smaller ships is useless," Wyrak said. "They're part of a hive mind. You have to destroy almost all of them before they stop functioning. Instead, you must focus on the big ships. That's where the hive mind is operating out of. But you have to do it in a hurry, or the smaller ships will destroy the planet you just came to save."

Jun shuddered at the wanton destruction that streaked across the screen. There were no big explosions—no oxygen in space. She still saw beams lighting out across the distance, some sort of laser, she assumed, cutting a swath through the small balls. The Lithic ships swam like salmon, upstream, racing to get at the behemoth above.

"After we destroyed a few of the Mind ships, the Bukoykan did stop their attacks for a short while. We had a few months' reprieve. Then they showed up again, this time, with three Mind ships present for every attack," Wyrak said. "Plus more escort ships that would defend the Mind ships."

"You said this has been going on for four years now?" Moe asked.

Wyrak nodded. "We won't survive for another four."

Jun had to agree. Those attacks were *savage*.

Was this enough evidence to get Humanity committed to the side of the Lithic?

Or would the court require more proof?

NINETEEN

Moe wasn't surprised by the quiet knock on his door after the Humans had left their meeting with Wyrak.

They were all spending the night on *The Roadrunner*. Atilio, Jun and Moe would go back to *Aisha* the next day, after everyone had had an opportunity to digest what Wyrak had showed them, and to start making plans.

The room that Dennis had provided Moe had a certain flair, of course. The walls themselves were a deep emerald green that Moe found surprisingly soothing. Gold accents highlighted the comfortable brown chairs and white counter edges. Thick black carpet covered the floor. Moe frequently kicked off his sandals and walked barefoot across it.

While Dennis complained about not being able to cover the walls in billowy silk fabrics to convey Moe's "princely" status, he'd still managed to talk someone (probably Atilio) into adding an entire collection of colorful pillows to the bed. Whenever Moe spent the night on *The Roadrunner* at least half of them ended up on the floor.

"Come in," Moe said, already trying to calm himself as Jun poked her head in.

"Are you busy?" she asked.

"Never too busy for you," Moe said simply as he sat up. It might have sounded like a line, but it was truly how Moe felt.

Jun gave him a grateful smile, closed the door behind her and walked all the way in.

Moe had been relaxing on the bed. Okay, possibly lounging on it, as he'd found the perfect combination of pillows that allowed him to be semi-prone while comfortable at the same time.

Jun joined him, sitting next to him on the bed but not too close. Tantalizing inches separated their shoulders.

They both stayed like that for a few moments, not saying anything.

"What do you think?" Jun asked eventually.

"I don't believe that this is a huge hoax, designed by Wyrak to trick Humanity into joining a war that isn't of their making," Moe said. "While possibly Atilio and Jamaal might not be convinced, that's just their own paranoia speaking. I believe Wyrak. I think the Lithic need help."

He sighed, then continued. "And I also think that it doesn't matter if we help the Lithic or not. We're next."

Jun let her head fall forward.

"What's wrong?" Moe asked.

"How do I convince Emperor Ogawa of the necessity? Let alone the Kollective?" She raised her head, but this time, let it thump against the wall. "I suppose all I have to do is place the correct bribes to get the Allied Worlds' to believe me. They'd jump at the chance to fight something. To prove their worth."

Moe nodded. While he didn't know the Emperor personally, and he stayed as far away as possible from anyone involved with the Kollective, the Allied Worlds' was just a collection of warlords, not a true governing force.

Given the amount of rampant corruption throughout Allied Worlds' space, he agreed that bribery might be all it would take to bring them onboard.

"What else do we need?" Moe said. "We can take a live alien to the Emperor. He can see all the evidence we've seen. Plus our recordings of the dead alien planet."

"I'm afraid it won't be enough. Wyrak would become a prisoner, just so scientists can study him. And we'll lose the Lithic when we could have saved them," Jun said.

Moe wondered at the bitterness of her tone.

"What would be proof enough? Do we need to capture one of the Bukoykan?" Moe said.

"According to Wyrak, the soldiers they send to fight don't have a lot of intelligence individually," Jun said. "And the tiny ships, well, they'll blow themselves up before we get them anywhere."

"Would two aliens help?" Moe had to ask. "If, in addition to Wyrak, we brought a second Lithic? One who'd survived an attack?"

"Wyrak's survived," Jun pointed out.

"No. Wyrak's part of the Lithic military," Moe pointed out. "He's seen battles. He hasn't been sitting in orbit, minding his own business, when a monster Mind ship appeared out of hyperspace and started spitting out the little ball ships."

"True," Jun said slowly. "I don't know how to find someone like that. Or how to convince them to come with us. Particularly when I can't guarantee that they'll be safe from us, at the end of all this."

"The problem seems insurmountable," Moe agreed. "That just means we have to break it down into smaller chunks. One bite at a time."

Jun shot him a puzzled look.

"According to my father, the only way to eat an elephant was one mouthful at a time," Moe explained. "Tiny chews."

"Death by a thousand cuts," Jun mused.

"I don't think that has the exact same connotations," Moe said dryly, "but yes, the same sort of idea."

They sat in silence for a few long moments. Moe thought he might be able to smell the floral perfume that Jun always wore.

Or perhaps that was just her own lovely scent.

"Will you hold me?" Jun asked in a very small voice, so softly Moe wasn't sure he'd heard her correctly.

"Of course," he said automatically.

He stayed very still with his arms open wide, giving Jun the opportunity to place herself gingerly against him, then abruptly collapsing and letting him take all her weight as she relaxed.

Very gently, Moe wrapped his arms around Jun.

Yes, that was her scent, very faintly floral. It might have haunted him some nights.

"It's going to be okay," Moe said as he rested his cheek against her soft hair.

Jun merely nodded and relaxed further.

Her breathing grew heavier and more even.

Moe couldn't help the smile that crossed his face as he realized she was starting to fall asleep.

He vowed to stay there with her, steady and strong, her bulwark to cling to, throughout the rest of these storms.

That was the sort of guy he was.

TWENTY

While Dennis might, perhaps, have been living his best dreams by being the *Envoy to the Galaxy*, what Rosey and the others wanted to do made *no sense* whatsoever!

"Get close to a battle? Are you nuts?" Dennis growled. "You do realize that I have no guns. No real shields either. We'd be a sitting groundhog!"

"Duck," Jamaal pointed out.

"Whatever. No. I don't agree," Dennis said.

All of the Humans and Wyrak were gathered together, sitting in the kitchen, with some of them around the table in the breakfast nook, others at a second table. (It absolutely *ruined* the aesthetics of the whole area! He was going to have to redo the room to balance out a longer seating area if people kept insisting on debasing his original design.)

Rosey reached out a hand and lightly touched Wyrak's arm.

Huh. Why was the alien starting to look so alarmed?

Surely not that nonsense about thinking machines taking over the galaxy.

Though if Dennis ever did have such pretensions, just imagine how fabulous everyplace would look!

"It's all right," she assured Wyrak. "He's just spouting off steam. He'll go where we ask him to go."

Wyrak still seemed bothered.

Dennis gave a loud sigh. "All right. Fine. We can go looking for a battle. As long as I stay on the edges! And no one starts shooting at us! If they do, we're gone."

"We just need some footage," Jamaal said. "Verified Human recordings of a fight. That will help us make our point with the Emperor."

"Wyrak, do you have some coordinates you can give me?" Dennis said, trying to show that he wasn't a sore loser. Really.

Wyrak just shrugged. "We never know where the Bukoykan are going to strike. And I don't want you just flying around our systems," he said.

Jun nodded at that. "I know. That would make me uncomfortable as well, having Lithic just showing up at our worlds."

"Do you have a gut feeling, Wrong-Way?" Atilio asked.

Wyrak appeared to be considering.

Dennis kept his sigh to himself, though it was so unfair. Not only did he have to pay attention to Human body language, now he had to learn Lithic as well!

"I'll work with Dennis. We'll figure out something," he said after a few moments.

"Of course we will," Dennis said. He was *Envoy to the Galaxy*. It was his job to ensure that whatever aliens or Humans had the privilege of riding with him had the best experience possible.

Plus, though no one had asked him about it, it was obvious that he now had a second, equally important job.

To save not just Rosey and the others, but everyone, everywhere.

Savior of the Galaxy didn't have as nice of a ring to it, but he'd make do.

Someone had to.

First thing Dennis and Wyrak worked on was to get the screens for the co-pilot in the helm of *The Roadrunner* to show Lithic numbers and words. Dennis even went so far as to manufacture a small keypad with the 3D printer that simulated the control board that Wyrak was used to.

After that, it became a guessing game. Wyrak would put in coordinates, Dennis would jump them there, and they'd look around.

Nothing to see, though. After a dozen hops, they were both getting frustrated.

Dennis nearly stopped Wyrak to ask which coordinates he meant when he plugged in the next set.

The navigator has said one set of numbers out loud.

However, he plugged a different set into the controls, reversing two of the strings of numbers.

They popped out at the edge of a battle.

"Enemy attacking!" Dennis shouted. "Get ready for evasive maneuvers!"

Though honestly, they all should have been strapped in for this. He still felt that giving a warning would be most polite.

"Are you recording this?" Rosey asked as she came running into the helm, sliding into the pilot's chair.

"Of course I am," Dennis said. That was the point of this entire exercise, why he was risking his skin. After just a few seconds though, he had to ask. "Are we done here? Can we go?"

He *hated* seeing this carnage. The Lithic military weren't present. No, it was just a bunch of merchant ships, massively outgunned, who were trying to make a stand around a space station.

Or had been.

Dennis had arrived at the end of the battle, and the small ball-like Bukoykan ships were already in retreat.

In less than five minutes, the three Mind ships jumped into hyperspace.

All that remained was wreckage.

"Is anyone alive?" Wyrak asked.

Though Dennis knew that the Lithic didn't cry tears, not like the Humans did, he still felt the heartbreak in those words.

"Scanning," Dennis said.

Mostly, it was just ship parts scattered around a now non-functioning space station that was already drifting toward the planet it had been orbiting. Probably had been a supply depot ten minutes ago.

"Wait. There's someone!" Dennis proclaimed.

He played the recording he was picking up on the ship's speakers. It was an automated message that roughly translated into, "Mayday! Mayday! Enemy attack!"

"Should I go get them?" Atilio asked. He was standing by, already ensconced in the least damaged of the two flitters carried by *The Roadrunner*. (The other still needed some work and Rosey didn't have the parts on the ship to fix it. Dennis was going to make sure that from now on they carried enough spare parts to fix *all* of his flitters.)

"Yes!" Wyrak said firmly.

"Sending the coordinates now," Dennis said.

Atilio sped off. Dennis switched one of the helm screens to show his progress, making it through the debris. More than once, Dennis did the equivalent of biting his tongue so he that didn't tell Atilio to *slow down* and *take better care of his equipment.* Particularly when, much to Dennis's surprise, Atilio managed to make it through the ugly mess out there *without* running into anything.

Of course, Dennis did end up directing Atilio, maneuvering the flitter's open compartment door so that the unpowered lifepod slid into the hold.

The screeching of metal as the pod settled in set Dennis's nerves on fire.

More damage!

Well, Rosey would just have to foot the bill on replacing *both* flitters when the time came.

As *Savior to the Galaxy*, he required better equipment.

She'd understand.

TWENTY-ONE

Jamaal found himself frustrated that Rosey didn't have a proper medical bay that he could visit. Instead, the unconscious Lithic merchant that they picked up was put into Wyrak's room, sealed away from everyone else.

Wyrak insisted that he be the first one she saw when she awoke. While Jamaal could understand the logic behind that, he still resented it.

"Hey."

The worry in Harkeen's voice brought Jamaal out of his stewing faster than anything else would have.

"I'm okay," Jamaal said, looking at his lover from across the table in the breakfast nook. He made himself take a deep breath and let it all out. "Really."

Harkeen reached across the table and patted Jamaal's hand, where it was wrapped tightly around his now cold tea.

"I know," Harkeen said with obvious amusement. "However, Rosey is lucky that those mugs are as sturdy as they are, or you would have cracked this one already."

Jamaal grimaced as he released the mug. Harkeen was right. He wasn't really in control of himself or his emotions. Probably hadn't been since they'd left the space station *Lorenzo*.

"Come on," Harkeen said, scooting out from under the table and standing. He reached out his hand for Jamaal. "I have an idea."

Jamaal nodded and reached up for that warmth he desperately needed, even when he didn't realize it.

So Jamaal may have been *slightly* disappointed when Harkeen didn't lead him to their room for more *reconnecting* as it were.

Instead, Harkeen took Jamaal to Rosey's exercise room, tugging him further into the room while staying close to the door. "Go on," Harkeen said. "Work it out."

Jamaal didn't say the words out loud. He knew that Harkeen would see the love in the smile he threw at the man.

When had anyone ever understood him as well? The short answer, as well as the long and intermediate ones were all the same.

Never.

Jamaal walked to the center of the room, then bowed deeply to Harkeen before he flowed into the first position.

Today felt like a slow day, where he breathed everything as much as felt it, stretching his limbs to their extremes as he slid from one position to the next, paying as much attention to the transitions as the "poses."

About midway through, Jamaal finally felt himself fully settled into his body again.

Originally, Jamaal had thought that bringing Harkeen with him on this adventure would be so that his trader persona would return more quickly, and the assassin wouldn't be dominant forever.

Now, he questioned if that was the case, or if Harkeen was somehow helping Jamaal *integrate* the two.

Though without a question, Jamaal the trader still had more fun.

Just as he was finishing up, Dennis announced, "Company coming."

Harkeen stayed where he was, and Jamaal continued going the

ending movements of his form as Wyrak and the female they'd rescued came through the door.

She was taller than Wyrak's six foot by just an inch. The majority of her fur appeared to be orange, though she wasn't striped like a domestic cat. Instead, she had patches of white that dotted the fur on her face, neck, and arms.

Her eyes widened at the sight of Jamaal, then she turned and practically stumbled into Wyrak when Harkeen cleared his throat, politely announcing his presence next to the door they'd just walked through.

Jamaal finished his form with a bow to his guests. "Hello," he said in the Lithic language.

"Hello," she said, her voice practically a soft purr.

"My name is Jamaal," he said, still in Lithic. "I am a Human male."

"My name is Kooron," she said. "I greet you."

"And I greet you," Jamaal said, bowing his head in a display of respect, or so Wyrak had taught them.

They all turned to Harkeen, who repeated the ritual.

Kooron turned to Wyrak and said something in rapid Lithic that Jamaal couldn't quite catch, but his assumed the gist of it went something along the lines of, "You weren't kidding, were you? More aliens!"

"Yes," Wyrak said. "But they will help."

Kooron just shook her head, obviously not believing him.

"What form were you doing?" Wyrak asked Jamaal.

"It's something we call *Tai Chi*, Yang-style," Jamaal told him. "Would you like to see it from the beginning?"

Wyrak paused before he pushed himself forward. "Teach me," he said.

Jamaal was surprised. Wyrak, for all that he was in the military, wasn't really a fighter. He was too geeky, too soft, too much in his head about numbers and ship coordinates and bright shiny stars.

"All right," Jamaal agreed. They started at the beginning, and

Jamaal went through the first half dozen positions with the transitions.

Wyrak followed along, obviously unused to moving his arms and legs in such a coordinated way.

As Jamaal had noted earlier, the Lithic had long arms, very long torsos, and short, almost stubby legs. When seated together at a table, Wyrak towered above all of them. The Lithic hand-to-hand combat forms were top heavy with many clawing attacks and few kicks.

It made sense, as the Lithic fingernails were naturally stronger and sharper than a Human's. Wyrak had mentioned having to keep his claws trimmed to civilized lengths instead of letting them grow pointed and sharp.

After going through the form a few times, Jamaal stood back and had Wyrak go through it on his own a couple of times. When he appeared to have a slight grasp on what he was doing, Jamaal turned to Kooron.

"Your turn," he told her.

"What?" Wyrak asked, sounding panicked.

"First you learn, then you practice, then you teach," Jamaal said stubbornly. "That's the best way to get it straight in your head."

Wyrak grumbled at him, while Kooron seemed amused.

Gracefully, she walked further into the room, standing in front of Wyrak, who seemed flustered all of a sudden.

"All right. We start here," Wyrak said. He tried to lead her through the dance, but for the first time, instead of turning to the left he turned to the right. He figured it out before Jamaal could point it out to him, and corrected himself.

After it happened a second time, Kooron finally spoke up. "Wrong-Way, huh?" she teased.

Jamaal couldn't help but grin at how that appeared to fluster the young male. "There's a reason for that," he said, shooting an evil glare at Jamaal.

Jamaal took a small step back and raised his hands, as if to say, *Hey, don't blame me for your two left feet.*

Though in the Lithic's case, that would probably be two right feet.

The three of them worked together, with Jamaal gently correcting his students now and again as they gained precision in the first section of the Yang Tai Chi form.

After an hour or so, they were all smiling and talking to each other, a combination of Human and Lithic common, with Dennis providing translations of words here and there as necessary.

Jamaal called a halt to their session, thanking the pair of them for all their hard work and attention.

They bowed in return, in that stiff, Lithic way.

Then Wyrak turned to Kooron and asked, "Are you ready to meet the others?"

Just a flash of worry crossed Kooron's face before she settled down and turned stubborn.

Oh, Jamaal liked her. And was going to have to be cautious around her as well. He recognized that stubbornness. Had possibly seen it a time or two in the mirror.

"Yes," Kooron said. "Not just the ones on this ship, but everywhere."

The pair of Lithic made their way out of the workroom while Dennis instructed everyone to meet in the kitchen.

Jamaal reached out a hand to Harkeen. He brought it up to his lips, kissing the back of it.

"Thank you," he said earnestly.

"For what?" Harkeen asked, obviously humoring him.

"For everything," Jamaal said as he felt himself grow even more steady.

It was time for one last council of war before they headed back in-system.

Back to the Human worlds.

TWENTY-TWO

The next leak about Project Red Elevator came a week later, and this time, it had *not* come from Duri.

She ran the information through a series of filters before finally picking Kipling Viteri as the probable culprit. He was one of those academics whose primary loyalties ran along the lines of science for the sake of science, as opposed to the Kollective. She had a vague recollection of a large man with a ruddy complexion and wild sandy-blond curls.

When he came marching into her office later that afternoon, she added that his suits were rumpled and probably second-hand, his large nose indicated that he regularly added brandy to his after-dinner cup of coffee, and he reminded her of a sullen hunting dog who didn't know who its master was.

Well, she was going to clear that up rather fast.

"So why did you decide to leak the information on Project Red Elevator?" Duri asked as soon as Kipling sat down.

She got a hearty, braying laugh as an answer.

Really, how rude.

"I'm assuming that you came to that conclusion after analyzing the content of the information?" he asked, still rather condescending.

"The meta-analysis of the sentence phrasing matches your papers with an eighty-eight percent accuracy," Duri said.

God, she hated the knowing smile that he gave her.

"Did it ever occur to you that someone may have just taken *my* work and decided to release it? Instead of their own, as a way to circumvent the watchers?" Kipling said.

Duri nodded. Of course that had occurred to her. "Except that it wasn't your work that was released. Or just your work," she added when he seemed about to object.

"But the majority of the leaked data was from my area of study," Kipling said. "The primary papers that the filters had to compare to were mine. So of course my name came up."

"Are you denying that you are responsible for this leak?" Duri said.

While the visitor chair that Kipling sat in wasn't equipped with heartrate monitors to help detect lies, Duri still felt confident in her own abilities.

However, this Kipling wasn't helping.

Kipling gave her a grin that was probably meant to be daredevilish or some such nonsense. "No," he said. "But I'm not saying I didn't help, either."

"So it's a conspiracy," Duri pronounced. "Against the direct orders of the Kollective government."

She was going to hang this smug bastard.

Kipling shrugged. "Information wants to be free. It's still a universal law. We pay for our entertainment, as we should. But actual facts are a universals that deserve to be shared."

Duri couldn't roll her eyes hard enough to express what she thought of that sentiment.

"And the information will be shared, 'made free' as you suggest, in due time," Duri pointed out. She'd agreed to that when she'd sequestered the scientists. There hadn't been a date put on the release, but even she knew that it couldn't remain exclusive to the Kollective forever.

That got her yet another knowing smile. "Perhaps. Perhaps not."

Duri knew better than to ask whether or not he trusted the Kollective. She understood that at best, their government was a Byzantine collection of fiefdoms, and navigating the ever-changing alliances was more difficult than playing chess while the pieces were constantly being swapped out.

"So who else is involved in this little conspiracy of yours?" Duri asked.

"I never claimed there was a conspiracy," Kipling replied. "You're the one who called it that. Not me."

Deflection. And a good one, actually. Kipling was rather good at dancing the fine line between lies and truth.

Then again, academic waters were almost as shark-filled as governmental ones.

Though in academia, the stakes were lower, the predators smaller, but the egos remained the same.

"Releasing the data before it's been fully analyzed is just hurting your own papers," Duri said, trying a different tactic.

"Actually, it isn't," Kipling said. For the first time, he appeared to be taking this seriously. "Science, true science, is all about collaboration. Someone else may spot something you don't see. They may have just read a paper that you haven't yet, be able to make connections that you can't. More eyes on the original source material is always a good thing."

Duri snorted. "And if they publish first?"

Kipling shook his head. "While yes, there is some undeniable cachet with that, the more accurate piece tends to be the one most remembered, as it will be the one that later generations quote."

"So this is about your legacy," Duri said. "You want to be remembered, your papers revered, far beyond your passing."

Kipling paused and considered. "While studying these materials, being the first on hand for the find of the millennium is not going to ensure that I'll be remembered, it will take more than that. Otherwise, I'm just a footnote in the history journals." He paused, then added, "Not that I'm saying that's my sole motivation."

"Motivation for what?" Duri said. Maybe she could catch this slimy bastard in some sort of lie.

"Merely for being thankful that I'm on this side of the grave," Kipling said. He abruptly stood. "Is there anything else?"

Duri looked up, quite stymied by this academic and not quite able to put her finger on why. "Are you responsible for the leak?"

"It was lovely chatting with you," Kipling said with a smile, followed by an extravagant bow. "I look forward to doing it again. Soon."

Then he walked out her door before she could even order him to sit back down.

Huh.

It took Duri most of the morning to figure out that the problem with Kipling, and possibly all the academics, was that they weren't afraid of her.

Well, she could fix that.

TWENTY-THREE

Though Ajax had managed to return to *Hermes 3.0* for a short while, he hadn't been allowed to stay there. Constantine had wanted him on the yacht for the upcoming battle.

Why? Ajax had no idea. He suspected it was because Constantine needed yet *another* person to flatter him and admire his brilliance as a fleet commander.

The warlord, for all his supposed brilliance, was really just a walking, talking bag of ego.

A part of him had to wonder if in addition, Constantine was also *conditioning* Ajax so he'd respond as the generals did when Constantine suggested some idiocy.

He'd wanted to become an important part of the warlord's operation.

Not at the cost of independent thought, though.

He tried to be smart about it. He slobbered over Constantine when the occasion called for it, all the while counting numbers in his head. He'd found that simple addition was the easiest way for him to stay clear of the obvious manipulation.

So far, it was working.

It might be a different story if he had to spend weeks over here on this damned yacht.

This meant that Ajax was almost relieved when they hopped into yet another fucking backwater of supposedly uninhabited space and were greeted with a battle.

He stood at the back of the helm, behind Constantine who was enthroned in the pilot's chair. It was the only part of the starship that was actually ship-like. Comforting electronics covered the walls, and the screens showed not just the space and stars in front of them, but side and back views of the yacht as well. The two subordinates who managed navigation and sensors/guns sat facing their great lord so they could always have the proper worshipfulness.

Of course, the air in here held that faint scent of flowers and the carpet was sinfully soft. The pilot's chair looked like a goddamned throne, with red leather padding and gold accents. Like the rest of the ship, the air was a touch too warm. Still, Ajax would have exchanged the stinking toga he was wearing for even a stretchsuit in a heartbeat.

Luck, or more likely, twisted fate, had them arrive just at the start of the destruction, as the small, ball-like ships had just begun pouring out of the black behemoth, heading toward the planet on the right of the screen.

Ajax hadn't really appreciated the sheer *size* of that beast. It was easily twice as long as the Kollective Defender that Constantine had. Possibly not as thick, though. It looked more like a wedge, composed of only one or two decks, unlike the Defender which floated through space like a goddamned city with multiple skyrises.

They had popped out into real space a little to the left and below the bigger ship.

"Attack! Attack!" Constantine shouted.

Ajax kept his snort to himself. So much for the military genius actually directing his forces.

Constantine's generals did as they were ordered, flowing over and up toward the huge target.

Menelaus was on the big Defender as well as being in charge

of several smaller fighters. Damocles, as befitted his name, had a more than a dozen long, knife-like ships that he commanded. Leonidas managed the rest of the rabble, a motley collection of fighters and transports. Odysseus and *Hermes 3.0* reported to Leonidas when it came to battle. While Ajax would have liked his ship to report directly to him, he wasn't high enough on the service pole. Plus, even he would admit that might be confusing during the middle of a battle.

Damocles's warriors went first, cutting a swath through the swarm of small alien ships. Leonidas and his crew followed behind, widening the path that Damocles had begun. Ajax cheered silently as he saw *Hermes 3.0* effectively destroy at least half a dozen of the smaller ball ships, all on its own.

He knew better than to point that fact out to Constantine. At least, not yet.

Menelaus trundled along afterward, the ships in his command taking out stragglers as they drew closer and closer to the big ship.

For a brief moment, Ajax thought they might actually have a chance. The Defender was within striking range of the mother ship. Had even sent a few disrupter bombs that way.

No one had anticipated not just one, but *two* additional streams of the little ships to flow out of the big ship. While the first batch had all flown out of what Ajax would call the bottom of the ship, these come out of the opposite side in two thin lines that curved around the front and back of the mother ship, heading toward the battle.

No, not directly toward the battle.

Behind the ships already approaching the behemoth.

"Fuck," Ajax said softly as Constantine started ordering his men. "Come around, idiots! Come around!"

Everyone had been so focused on the prize in front of them that none of them had been watching their flanks or their back.

The ball-like ships flew toward Constantine's fleet like a buzzing hive of black bees, intent on devouring all the prey in its path.

As the Defender was the first large ship in their path, the smaller ships converged on it, practically blocking it from view.

No single little ball-shaped ship was capable of doing that much damage. There were just so damned many of them. It reminded Ajax of a recording he'd once seen of a type of man-eating fish, and how they'd stripped the flesh from their much-larger victim.

Alarms rang through Constantine's helm. Red lights flashed.

For a moment, Ajax was afraid that they'd fallen under attack as well, but it was just the warning system alerting them to the fact that the Defender was about to be obliterated.

Once Constantine's biggest ship was gone, the other ships didn't stand a chance.

Constantine continued yelling at his generals, telling them to attack, to defend themselves.

Hell, he even ordered them to return to him. Not in a retreat, no, but to protect him.

Ajax found himself detached from the devastation, as if he were watching a recording of something, not that it was happening directly in front of them.

The generals were getting conflicting orders from their warlord. As they'd been conditioned to respond, their behavior grew erratic as different demands were placed on them.

A coordinated attack might have eventually won out over the black beast.

Instead, it was a slaughter.

Ajax froze further when *Hermes 3.0* broke apart, as though giant hands had taken hold of the front and back of the ship and gentle torn it into two.

The little ball-ships also cleaned up the mess they left behind. No lifepods were allowed to escape whole.

Constantine realized his own danger about the same time Ajax did, ordering the yacht to retreat.

They slipped out of the system before any of the ball-like ships even fired at them.

The black lines outlining all the edges of the helm jarred Ajax out of his detached state. Strange how hyperspace brought him to real space.

His hand shook. Sweat drenched his back. Despite the heat of the helm, he was shivering with cold.

Shock, some distant part of his mind told him.

Constantine turned his chair around to face Ajax. His eyes were glazed, his jaw slack. Even his perfect skin looked pale and waxy.

The warlord shook himself, as if suddenly realizing that he had an audience.

Ajax gulped as those eye pinpointed him, nailing his feet to the carpet. He tried to stop trembling, but his hands wouldn't obey.

Constantine stood up and strode over so he loomed above Ajax.

"You will tell *no one* of what just happened," Constantine growled.

Ajax felt the manipulation stirring his soul.

He nodded and stammered, somehow managing to put on a show of obedience.

"No, lord, of course not. What was there to see, anyway? But the disobedience of your generals," Ajax said, feeling his tongue taking over and saying things even though he hadn't told it to.

That got him the ghost of a smile.

"Good," Constantine said. "That's exactly what occurred. My generals tried to ambush me. Mutiny against me."

The thought planted itself firmly in Ajax's brain, though his eyes hadn't seen anything to that account.

"Fools," he whispered, his tongue still moving of its own accord.

Constantine patted his cheek gently.

Ajax felt himself lean into the touch even as he cursed his body for betraying him so. It was just that Constantine was warm, while he was very, *very* cold.

Then Constantine swept out of the helm, probably to console himself over his loss in the arms of one (or more) of his dancing girls.

Ajax stayed on the helm until he felt as though he could walk without falling, his legs stable again and no longer shaking.

How long did he have before Constantine decided that he, too, was a liability?

TWENTY-FOUR

Atilio joined the others in the kitchen for the last "council of war" they would hold before they went back to the Human worlds.

He shared a smile with Rosey at Dennis's sighs and apologies to his guests for how they had *ruined* the space by bringing the extra table in there.

Kooron introduced herself to everyone, seeming slightly overwhelmed by the sheer number of aliens that she was having to meet at the same time.

Though no one translated the exchange that Kooron and Wyrak had at the end of that, Atilio thought the gist was somewhere along the lines of, "And you came here voluntarily? Without anyone else? You're either braver or stupider than I thought."

Atilio had to concur.

Then again, he suspected that if the situation were reversed, Rosey might have gladly sacrificed herself, gone off on the adventure of a lifetime with the Lithic. Probably would have already arranged a racing circuit for them.

And he would have gone with her, if she'd asked.

They were still dancing around the topic. Atilio understood

her hesitance. He had a life tied to a different ship. She wasn't about to give up everything to follow him.

Until their destinations changed, they'd probably stay in their separate lanes.

All of the people had already sat down around the tables with their beverages of choice when Rosey asked Moe where Jun was.

"She said she'd be right here," Moe said with a frown.

"I can go get her," Atilio said, standing. He was on the outer edge of the second table and in an easy position to hop up to fetch and carry for the rest of the more important players.

Jun burst into the kitchen before he had a chance to do more than that, though.

"Greetings!" Jun said as she came up to the table. Her Lithic was better than the rest of theirs, though Jamaal's was a close second.

She introduced herself, with Wyrak adding some words to make sure that Kooron understood Jun's place in one of the three Human governments.

Kooron's eyes widened comically when she understood that Jun was *royalty*. It was an old-fashioned system of government for the Lithic, but it had turned out that every culture had fairy tales about princesses.

"Have you explained to her about Dennis? And Sano?" Jun asked as she sat down.

Wyrak shook his head. He sighed, looked down for a moment, then started a rapid-fire string of Lithic that Atilio couldn't follow.

He did understand Kooron's initial response.

"WHAT?"

Dennis came in at that point, trying to soothe the aliens.

How to explain that he was just a goofball and a frustrated interior designer and had no intention of taking over anything? He had enough problems running Rosey's life (or so he'd complained to Atilio on more than one occasion). He did *not* want the headaches that would come with trying to run entire worlds of Humans.

Ugh.

Eventually, though Kooron still appeared skeptical, she accepted Wyrak's explanation. For now.

Jun started the conversation again.

"The reason I'm late is because we've been putting together more of the Atoylee papers," she said.

That brought up a whole additional side conversation about how there were *other* aliens out there, though they'd been destroyed. Dennis helpfully provided pictures for that, the lovely sunflower-like people as well as their destroyed world.

Atilio had seen the footage of the moonbase, and couldn't help but admire it again, particularly as Dennis did a split-frame and showed the base as they'd found it, compared to the base as it had once been.

Finally, when everyone was caught up, Jun continued.

"Sano's been doing a deep dive on all the Atoylee papers. They were fighting an alien species that they called the Bukoykan."

She paused, then added, "We don't know if these are the same aliens that you're currently fighting. We have reasons, now, to believe they might be."

Atilio took a deep breath at that.

If that really was the case, then the Bukoykan were *ancient*.

Why were they still attacking other species? Or were they just that warlike?

"On the Atoylee moonbase, they were developing chemical weapons to stop the Bukoykan," Jun continued. "The problem is that it's all chemical signatures, and it's been very difficult to map their system to ours. Sano thinks she's finally figured out a translation."

Jun paused and Sano took over.

Atilio noticed that both Lithic stiffened at the sound of Sano's voice over the ship's speakers.

Was there a way to lessen that? Maybe she could speak out of the necklace that Jun always wore, that contained most of the AI?

Except that would probably freak them out more. Maybe an image on a screen? As long as it looked robotic?

"The Atoylee were masters when it came to combining chemicals, arranging chemical bonds, breaking and rejoining them," Sano said.

While she spoke in Lithic, Dennis translated for the rest of the poor slobs around the table.

"They had come up with two solutions that passed their tests," Sano continued. "They appeared to either have gathered samples of cell material from the Bukoykan, or they were able to somehow deduce their chemical makeup."

"Did they join with the Bukoykan? Agree to become part of the galactic empire? And then change their minds?" Atilio mused. He started when everyone turned to him.

Oops. Hadn't meant to speak that out loud.

"It's possible," Sano said. "Either that, or they were shown the process of being *converted* and reverse engineered it."

Wyrak spoke up. "Our scientists were shown enough data that they thought the process might work. It changed the brain, grew an additional organ there, so that we could talk and hear the Mind."

"Our people couldn't reverse engineer the process," Kooron added, obviously not wanting to be left out of the conversation.

"The Atoylee, though they weren't as mechanically advanced, and they hadn't discovered hyperspace, were much more sophisticated chemically than the Bukoykan probably gave them credit for," Sano said.

"Interesting," Jamaal commented.

Atilio and the others all nodded in unison.

"Some of this is just conjecture," Sano warned. "But the Atoylee mention two different types of starships. One was small and round. They compared them to bees."

Both Wyrak and Kooron nodded.

Huh. Seemed that they had a similar insect, though the name was different.

"The big ships, the ones you call the Mind ships, they called Hive ships," Sano said. "They appeared to understand that there wasn't anything you could do about the Bees. The main focus of their attack was the Hive. Now, you said before that the Bukoykan grow their ships?"

"Yes," Wyrak and Kooron said simultaneously.

Wyrak immediately leaned back and indicated that Kooron should continue.

Right. Semi-matriarchal society.

"The inside of a Mind ship is mostly hollow. The sides are lined with vines that Bee ships grow from." She gave a shudder that quite frankly, everyone at the table repeated. "At the beginning of a battle, those vines start popping out Bee ships, complete with a Bukoykan warrior, by the dozens."

"Thank you," Sano said. "That puts a better light on these results. Their first weapon was a bomb that, when detonated, deployed a chemical that disrupted all organic bonds. Specifically, anything that's got the organic signature of the Bukoykan."

Atilio sat back, blinking with surprise.

That...wasn't something that he wanted falling into the hands of just anyone. Even if it currently only worked on the Bukoykan. People were clever, and might be able to reverse engineer it to do the same for anything organically Human.

Or Lithic.

"It didn't last for long. They were very concerned about mutation, so they had a 'kill gene' enclosed in it. They also concentrated on making it a contained blast. But they believed that it would be enough to take out one of the Hives," Sano said.

"Were they ever able to test it?" Jamaal asked, looking so serious that Atilio had to stop himself from leaning back and away from the man.

"That's the problem," Sano said. "They weren't as advanced

mechanically, or with weapons. While I believe the chemistry is solid, they had no delivery mechanism."

"We could fix that," Atilio said dryly. Hell, given a free afternoon, he could probably redneck something together with just the spare parts on the two starships.

Before anyone could take him up on it, Sano continued.

"Then there's the second weapon. Do either of you know of a place called just *Bukoy*?"

While Kooron shook her head no, Wyrak tilted his head from side to side.

Kooron shot him a glare. Wyrak shrugged.

"In the *Bukoykan* language, the term *kan* is roughly equivalent to the word for 'people,'" he explained. "The other races we visited, who'd been brought into the Mind, all had that term affixed to their names. We would have become the Lithickan."

"Do you think *Bukoy* was the name of their home planet? Or system?" Jun speculated.

"It's possible," Wyrak said. "But I don't know for certain. I don't know if anyone in the high command would know either."

After a pause, Sano continued. "The Atoylee had a second weapon that was destined for a place called *Bukoy*. It was similar to the first, except that it wasn't short range, and it wouldn't stop after so many generations of cell formations. It would keep going, keep spreading, eating everything that it touched."

"A planet killer?" Atilio asked sharply.

Boy, he *really* didn't want that sort of knowledge getting out.

"I think so," Sano said. "It's possible that the Bukoykan also thought so. We've always believed that the Atoylee had more organic cities and buildings. What if there were more stone, concrete, and metal? But the Bukoykan made absolutely certain that nothing of the Atoylee survived?"

"Then we might have a true weapon on our hands," Jamaal said.

Was that grim satisfaction? Fear? Or a combination of both?

Atilio wasn't sure how he felt about the Atoylee now. Those

beautiful sunflower-like people, who'd evidently not just contemplated genocide, but developed the weapons to do it.

Then again, they were facing their own extinction. They probably would have gone through with it. However, they'd run into hurdles that they couldn't surmount.

Like no true starships, no access to hyperdrive. No way to deliver their doom.

"So what do we do now?" Sano asked.

The entire group was silent for a few moments, contemplating the massive discoveries they'd made, and trying to figure out how to use them without potentially killing everyone in the galaxy.

Or at least that was what Atilio was thinking about.

They needed to be able to use this weapon without any of the governments getting their sticky little fingers into it.

But how?

TWENTY-FIVE

Rosey *really* wasn't happy with the plan that they'd come up with.

She'd still agreed to it in the end, because it did make sense for them to "divide and conquer" as it were. They'd meet up afterward.

She tried to look at the bright side. It meant more time with Atilio on *Aisha*, even if the pair of them were frequently rolling their eyes at the moroseness of Moe and his sadness at being separated from his princess.

They also had a sliver of Sano with them, as she was the one who could explain all the chemistry.

The others...well, they had their own missions to accomplish.

Rosey didn't know any pure chemists. She knew people who were metallurgists, like Lloyd. So here they were, going to meet another of Jamaal's questionable contacts.

Fortunately, he'd insisted that they meet him at the ass-end of nowhere, not on a planet or space station. That certainly worked in their favor, as *Aisha* was still a wanted ship.

Moe had plopped them into real space about an hour ago. Rosey had spent the time tinkering in one of the workshops with

Atilio, trying to come up with the perfect delivery device for this weapon of theirs.

The solution they'd developed was fairly inspired. It was also something that the Lithic military couldn't have devised, or possibly even considered, as they didn't use thinking machines in their starships.

"You better get up here," Moe said as they were putting the last touches on their first prototype.

"Coming," Rosey said. She and Atilio went quickly up to the helm.

A huge starship floated in front of them, a little off the port side.

It looked like someone had taken the hull of a Kollective Defender, then added row upon row of bright blue-white lights, starting at the keel and working upward. It *twinkled* against the black sky. Several towers jutted off the top, like old-fashioned chimneys.

Rosey rolled her eyes at it. Yup. She could instantly tell it was a J4 design—a set of four cloned brothers who did extravagant spaceships. She could tell from the lights as the lens flair that they were famous for flashed across the screens.

Moe looked at her from the captain's chair, starting to rise up out of it.

Rosey waved him back down. Though she was nominally in charge of this farce, she didn't want Moe to feel as though she was taking over.

"It's a nice day for a parade," Rosey broadcast, using the code words that Jamaal had given her.

"Too bad the forecast says rain," came a chipper voice in return.

"Bring your umbrella?" Rosey asked. "The blue one?"

"And the red one as well."

Rosey nodded, the code phrases having been satisfied.

"Do you want to come over and share it?" was the next statement.

Rosey glanced first at Atilio, then Moe. She grinned when they shrugged in unison.

"Sure," Rosey said. "I'll be bringing one person with me," she warned, nodding at Atilio.

"Good thing my umbrella's big enough for three," the voice replied. "Use the open docking bay."

"We got ourselves a date," Rosey informed Atilio.

"You know I'm not into threesomes, right?" he teased.

Rosey snorted at him. "As if you'd be that lucky," she retorted.

That got her a grin before they all turned serious again, looking back at Moe.

He nodded at them. "Sano will keep us in contact," he said, repeating the plan that they'd already worked out, "I'll go back and inform the others if you don't return after three hours."

"No stupid heroics," Atilio warned.

Moe gave them a sad smile. "Not now, no," he said. "But if he does take you, well, there aren't many places where he can hide. You will be avenged."

Rosey didn't roll her eyes as much as she might have wanted to. Angry and vengeful didn't sit well on Moe's shoulders.

He wasn't *that guy*, as he'd frequently said.

Still, it was nice to know that someone might try to appease their angry ghosts.

Rosey let Atilio fly the flitter from *Aisha* over to the overly-decked-out starship. Officially, his role was her subordinate.

Unofficially? Bodyguard. While his weapons weren't obvious, he was still armed.

And dangerous. Jamaal had seen to that, taking the engineer under his wing and expanding his knowledge of weapons and martial forms during their time together.

The docking bay—the black, gaping hole that showed up

toward the bottom of the ship—was more than big enough for the little flitter. Absolutely no challenge for a pilot like Atilio.

Still, he appeared to be showing off a little as he floated the little ship into the hold, then landed it so gently Rosey couldn't feel when they'd stopped moving.

He gave her a cheeky grin.

She just rolled her eyes at him, while at the same time, marking off yet another box on her checklist of things that she was going to miss when he went off with Moe.

Sensors pronounced that the air outside was breathable. Rosey was still in her signature stretchsuit, made of a shiny, rosy color with her initials embroidered over the heart. Atilio was also in a stretchsuit, but from *Aisha*, matte gray with the colors of the Empire—green and gold—embroidered around the cuffs and collar.

They could call up their helmets in an instant if the air suddenly became not-breathable, though Jamaal didn't think that this contact would use the same trick twice.

A single man awaited them close to the door of the hold. He was slight—possibly not much taller than Jun's five feet. His face was more tan than Jun's, as well as more angular, though he had the same black hair that she did, cut short. More likely Chinese ancestry than Japanese. From a distance, his eyes appeared steely. He also wore a stretchsuit, red with black accents highlighting the chest.

It wasn't until they were up close that Rosey saw his genetic modifications. Or at least she thought it might be genetic, though it might be cybernetic.

Dr. Wu's eyes weren't just steely. They appeared to be made out of steel, bright and metallic.

What could he see through such eyes? What measurements was he taking of them? Or was the enhancement primarily to aid him in his chemical concoctions?

"Greetings, fair guests!" he called as they walked across the floor of the hold. "I am Dr. Wu. Welcome to my factory ship."

After Rosey and Atilio had introduced themselves, their host told them, "Come. I have a meeting room ready."

He led them down a fairly standard hallway, with gray metallic walls and black rubber coating on the floor.

Rosey could already hear Dennis's complaints about how *beige* it all was.

The meeting room was only large enough to hold four around a small, brown table. Screens filled every wall.

Rosey was happy that she wasn't claustrophobic, as they fit around the table tightly.

"Can I offer you some refreshments?" Dr. Wu said.

"No, thank you," Rosey said primly.

Jamaal had warned them not to accept any food or drink from Dr. Wu. While he probably wouldn't poison them, that didn't mean he wouldn't try something on them. Like turning their piss bright blue.

However, her response just made Dr. Wu chuckle. "I see Jamaal has already warned you," he said.

Rosey shrugged. She wasn't about to deny it.

"So, how can I help my dear friend Jamaal?" Dr. Wu said.

"What we're about to show you needs to be kept to yourself," Rosey warned. It was one of the things that all the conspirators had agreed upon.

"You wound me, my lady," Dr. Wu responded. "Why would I ever share one of my personal creations with a competitor?"

Rosey nodded. Jamaal had said that Dr. Wu might respond that way. "Still, I need your promise."

Dr. Wu narrowed his eyes at Rosey. "Did Jamaal tell you why I agreed to meet with you?"

"Something about a favor," Rosey said. "Jamaal wasn't too forthcoming about the details."

That earned her a smile. "I was accused of poisoning someone. Someone who I hadn't actually killed. One of my rivals tried to frame me." Dr. Wu shook his head. "Jamaal was the only one who believed me when I claimed my innocence. He went out of his way to help me. I have owed him a favor ever since."

Rosey had to admit she was slightly surprised. Even Serious Jamaal had never struck her as the "avenging angel" type. He went in and got the job done, heedless of where the bodies fell. Or the number of them.

"So while it would go against my general principles to tell anyone else of this work, it would also go against my bond with Jamaal," Dr. Wu said seriously. "He has kept my secrets for over a decade. I will take his to my grave."

That mollified Rosey. She glanced at Atilio, who also nodded.

"Besides," Dr. Wu added after a moment. "He's the only one who would also track me to the ends of the galaxy if I betrayed him. And be successful at it."

That also reassured Rosey.

"So, what we have for you are two chemical compounds. The first needs to be delivered in some sort of aerosol that will work in zero-g. The second needs to be activated on detonation, and not before," Rosey explained.

She unzipped a pocket on her sleeve and pulled out a standard data chip, then handed it to Dr. Wu.

He plugged it into a console on his side of the table. After a few moments of verifying that nothing on the chip would harm his computer systems, he pulled up the chemical composition of the first weapon.

The room darkened slightly and delicate molecules floated on the screens, showing first one then the next, and then how they combined.

"Interesting!" he exclaimed after a few moments of study. "These are not standard chemical bonds or arrangements."

"We know that," Rosey said dryly. "That's why we came to you, the expert."

"Do you understand what this chemical will do? In the right circumstances?" Dr. Wu said after a few more moments.

Rosey shrugged. "We think so. Yeah."

Dr. Wu shut down the screen holding the floating chemical structure. The room was suddenly much darker. Dr. Wu's silver eyes flashed at them.

"And Jamaal believes that this is necessary?" Dr. Wu asked.

"We all do," Rosey said firmly.

Her heart suddenly started beating louder in her chest.

Was this professional poisoner going to turn away their business? Refuse to honor Jamaal's favor?

Were they going to have to shoot their way out of here? She felt Atilio tense beside her. Though he wasn't a violent man, she knew that if anything happened to her the galaxy would shudder in the face of his vengeance.

"I will do it," Dr. Wu said, bringing the screens back live again. "It is an interesting problem, and I do owe Jamaal a favor."

He paused, then added, "But we are even after this. I do not owe him or anyone else anything."

"Agreed," Rosey said. She knew that Jamaal had been willing to give up his favor this way, that he would no longer have any hold on this man.

"All right," Dr. Wu said. "This will take me a few days. May I keep this?" he said, holding up the data chip.

"Please, do," Rosey said.

Did he know that she'd embedded an ITT into the plastic casing? That unless he enclosed the chip in something that completely blocked all transmissions, it would broadcast his location?

"This will take me a few days," Dr. Wu admitted. "I will first need to manufacture the chemicals, as none of these naturally occur. Then I'll have to come up with the best procedure to ensure their bonding. Do you want to wait here? Or over on your ship?"

"We'll wait here," Rosey said. "Don't worry about entertaining us. We have our own supplies on the flitter."

That just got her a grin. "Damn. Jamaal spoiled all my fun. Suit yourselves, though."

He escorted them back to the hangar where their flitter sat, unmolested as far as Rosey could tell.

Now, they just had to wait. And see if the genius that Jamaal had believed in would actually work in their favor.

TWENTY-SIX

Humans were *weird*. They smelled funny and the lights and colors they preferred hurt Wyrak's eyes. They had strange habits, showed their teeth too often, were far too solitary, and didn't understand pack mentality at all.

Plus, he was *so tired* of the military rations that he had to eat. They'd found a few foods that he appeared to tolerate, but the tastes were still off.

Fortunately, he hadn't had to share his ever dwindling supply with Kooron. The lifepod they'd picked up had had its own stash, along with a set of inhalers.

Wyrak had assumed that when they picked up Kooron that she'd be assigned the same suite as him, that they'd share the space.

It had taken more than a little bit of firm instructions on his part to make that happen. The Humans had assumed that she'd want her own room.

After all, they all slept separately, except for Jamaal and Harkeen.

And it wasn't as if Wyrak was going to try to *mate* with this female. They didn't know each other, or each other's packs. That would just be rude. His own packmates would turn against him if he tried something so heinous.

Again, Humans were weird.

Having another of the Lithic there would ease his soul. And hers. The Lithic weren't meant to be alone. There had always been speculation that the Bukoykan had only made their offer of merging because the Lithic were pack creatures, and so could more easily conceive of such an outcome.

Kooron turned out to be about ten years his senior and *constantly* teased him. Worse than his milk-mother had. Almost every suggestion he made received a derisive comment.

Like that morning, when he'd been shocked at her request to Dennis to turn down the air filters in their shared room.

Though he knew that Dennis (and maybe others) were listening, he still hissed at her. "Don't tell them things that might be considered a weakness!"

Kooron rolled her eyes at him. "Look. Either we get to stay here and be comfortable, or they're going to kill us, dissect us, and find out anyway. I'd rather be comfortable, and not go out of my way to be a hero. Is that all right with you?"

Wyrak sighed. Maybe she was right. It would be good to have less air filtering, so that the room smelled like *theirs* and not so much like a sterile, Human place.

"Dennis?" Kooron said with a wicked gleam in her eyes that Wyrak didn't trust. "Do you think you could do something about the lights as well?"

"Certainly!" came Dennis's enthusiastic reply. "What would you like?"

The three of them spent the morning warming up the lights, toning down some of the whites and blues, adding more orange to it. The white ceiling suddenly became tolerable.

"Do you want me to change the lights in the rest of the ship?" Dennis inquired as they finally came up with their preferred combination.

It surprised Wyrak when Kooron looked to him for an answer.

"No," Wyrak said slowly. "I think just in here, making it more homey for us, is sufficient."

"I aim to please, and to make all my guests truly comfortable," Dennis gushed.

"Okay, thank you," Wyrak said. "We're going to talk together now."

"Just say my name if you want anything, anything at all. Now, I'm going to give you some privacy," the ship said.

There wasn't the sense of a presence being withdrawn. Wyrak had no idea if Dennis was really no longer listening to them or not.

"He is a thinking machine?" Kooron asked, as if she needed to verify.

"So I've been told," Wyrak said. "Him and Sano."

"They aren't like the ones in our history," Kooron continued. "They appear more helpful than overreaching. Unless you want to count their willingness to help as being pushy."

Wyrak nodded. That had been what it felt like to him as well. The AIs still made him uncomfortable sometimes, but he accepted that the Humans appeared to have tamed the digital beasts.

"What do you know about this person we're going to meet?" Kooron asked.

That devolved into a long, *long* discussion about what it meant to be a spy.

The Lithic had the concept, but it mostly occurred in fiction. It was very difficult to betray one's pack. Even more difficult to infiltrate a tightly-knit pack.

While the Lithic could lie to one another, again, it was difficult to do. A constant liar had a scent. The ones who were like chameleons, able to shift alliances quickly because they never felt a pack connection with anyone, were never full trusted in the first place because they smelled wrong.

As part of Wyrak's military training, he'd been taught how to scent these individuals.

The very, *very* few who did occur outside of fiction tended to be psychopaths and didn't last too long.

That was part of the problem with the thinking machines. They had no scent. It was impossible to know if they told the truth. It sometimes surprised Wyrak that they'd ever been trusted at all.

Then again, people *were* lazy, and it was much easier to have a machine do everything instead of doing those things themselves.

Eventually, Wyrak was able to get across the concept that Jamaal had been some sort of honorable spy and that they were going to meet with his commander.

"They're all criminals, aren't they?" was Kooron's response.

"Possibly," Wyrak admitted.

"Wrong-Way, I hope you know what you're doing."

He just shrugged. "We won't know until we get there, to the end of this journey." He paused, then added, "If you really want to leave, to make your way back to our systems, I'm sure they'd help you."

"What, are you calling me a coward?" Kooron responded. "Do you think I don't have the nerve to follow through with this?"

"No, no!" Wyrak said, immediately backing down. "I didn't mean that at all!" He sighed. Nothing he said was ever right.

That just got him a snort. "Ah, you're too easy to wind up," Kooron said.

Wyrak glared at Kooron, who gave him an unrepentant grin. "If we manage to get through this all with our fur intact, we're going to be heroes for our people," she said seriously.

As far as Wyrak could tell, the concept of *hero* was slightly different in Human terms. For them, it meant a solitary great leader. In Lithic, that was true, but it was more of a leader of the pack rather than a single person.

"You will be," Wyrak grumbled. There was no doubt who the high command, as well as the rest of the population, would assume was the leader of their two-person pack.

"Awww, I'll give you credit for things. Some," Kooron teased.

Wyrak rolled his eyes. Before they could continue with their banter, Dennis sounded a soft bell in the suite.

That was a much better way to let the Lithic know that their presence was requested, rather than Dennis announcing it. While Wyrak and Kooron didn't like being alone, they did need time with just the pair of them, a more true pack.

"We'll make it back home," Kooron assured him. Or possibly both of them.

"We will. We'll steal a ship if we need to. I can get us there."

That just got him a sly smile. "I guess you do have your uses," Kooron said before she glided out of the room.

Wyrak followed. For all that he was a pack navigator, third class, all he really did was to point the way for others, so that they could go together.

He wasn't cut out to be a solo operator.

None of the Lithic were.

TWENTY-SEVEN

There wasn't much for Moe to do alone on *Aisha*. He was glad that Rosey and Atilio had stayed over on Dr. Wu's ship, though, as the mad chemist had had many questions for them about dispersal of the agent.

After four days, they'd gathered back together. Dr. Wu's floating city disappeared into hyperspace first, followed shortly by *Aisha*.

Once they'd reached hyperspace, Atilio pulled out his handy scanner that found trackers. It surprised all three of them that Dr. Wu hadn't put any sort of trackers on the chemicals that he'd entrusted to them.

Maybe he didn't want to be implicated in whatever happened to them. Or perhaps he just didn't want to know.

He'd supplied them with vats of the stuff. It made Moe uncomfortable every time he used that hallway, knowing what was locked away.

He was a merchant who dealt with trade goods, not an arms dealer.

"Ya know, the brood is getting might strong in here," Atilio said as he plopped down beside Moe in the kitchen.

"I know," he said, sighing. He paused, then couldn't help but ask, "Are we sure we're doing the right thing?"

Atilio paused before answering. "I think we are," he said softly. "I've gone over the recordings we have of the Bukoykan attack. Once they find us, they aren't going to just stop. They're going to attack, and keep attacking, until every Human planet resembles Niani."

"I don't mind that we've developed weapons that can stop one of their ships," Moe said, feeling his way through the subject. "But that planet killer…"

Atilio sighed. "I know. I worry about that as well. First of all, we don't know if it'll work. Dr. Wu believes that it will, but he also had to adjust the original formula to better weaponize it. So it would never be a first line of defense."

"It still makes me nervous," Moe admitted.

"You know that we don't have the actual formula that Dr. Wu arrived at, right?" Atilio said. "He claimed he had to use proprietary chemicals to make it. Rosey was just as happy to let him have it. So even if it works, we can't mass produce it out of hand. We'd have to go back to Dr. Wu and prove our case."

Moe wasn't sure if that made him feel better or not. "So our fate may lie in the hands of a mad scientist?"

Atilio grinned at him. "Hasn't it always, to one extent or another? Some insane genius could always whip up total chemical warfare and decide to unleash it on the unsuspecting worlds. It sometimes surprises me that Humanity has managed to survive this long without blowing ourselves up."

Moe had to admit that had occurred to him already. "Do we know if the other formula, the ship killer, works?"

"Only in theory," Atilio said with a shrug. "And if it doesn't work, we're in real trouble. However, we do have the improved formula for that."

"Convenient that," Moe remarked dryly.

"Aye," Atilio said. "Look, I was in the military. I wouldn't hand over either formula to the generals, no matter how much they begged. But I firmly believe that the Lithic need the help to at least stop the attacks, so we can force the Bukoykan to talk."

"And what if they tell us that the Lithic are the aggressors?" Moe said.

"It's possible that the Lithic military and their powers that be have been lying to the rest of the population this entire war. Unlikely, though," Atilio said. "It's too extravagant of a con for someone to pull off. Plus, Lithic have a thing about telling lies."

"Jun has speculated that because their sense of smell is so good, they might be able to detect by smell when someone is lying to them," Moe said.

"Exactly," Atilio said. "Plus, even if they got a sample of the planet-killer goo, they probably wouldn't be able to reverse-engineer it."

"Can we?" Moe asked.

"Sano might be able to if she was given the right equipment and time. Others? Probably not, because they have no idea what the base chemical structure from the Atoylee was," Atilio said.

Moe wouldn't say that he was at ease with any of this. He had to trust the people around him, that they wouldn't be easily pushed into killing planets.

He took a sip of his now-tepid tea and grimaced. He raised his eyebrows at Atilio and lifted his mug.

Atilio nodded and smiled his thanks as Moe rose and fixed them both something better to drink.

When Moe sat back down, Atilio asked, "So. If we're successful here. If we stop a war from starting, and live through introducing the Lithic to the galaxy. And if we manage to get the warrants off our ass. What's next, after that?"

Moe sighed and nodded. He hadn't really allowed himself to do a lot of thinking about the far future and all those what ifs.

"In an ideal galaxy, my pie-in-the-sky best scenario," Moe started, "we succeed, we survive, and we prosper. Before we left *Nightfall*, I'd already identified a few areas of trade that we could provide to the Lithic."

"Going to set up your own trading empire?" Atilio teased.

"That's the plan," Moe said. He knew it was a grand ambition, to become the primary trade partner between the Lithic and the Humans.

But maybe, *maybe,* that would give him enough money and status to be able to openly pursue Jun.

"Why?" Moe asked. "What's next for you, if we succeed?"

It was Atilio's turn to sigh and look down at his hands and the mug of tea he held.

"Would you like your own fleet of ships to manage?" Moe said. Because honestly, that was what he'd love, for Atilio to remain his right-hand man and to manage large parts of his empire. He could trust Atilio to do the right thing.

"What, you going corporate on me?" Atilio said with a grin. He paused, taking a sip of his tea, before he responded. "Sounds too much like work," he eventually quipped.

"We could set up a local hub centered around the space station *Lorenzo,*" Moe offered. Would that be enough to get Atilio to bite?

Atilio just shook his head no. "Too much paperwork, not enough getting my hands dirty."

"What if instead of trade goods, it was technology? Trying to adapt Lithic ship designs to our own, and vice versa?" Moe said.

That got Atilio's attention. "Maybe," he said after a bit. "But you'd have to base that closer to a ship-building hub, which *Lorenzo* is not."

That just made Moe smile. "We'll see," he said.

If he was going to dream, may as well dream really big, right?

Not just turn himself into *that guy,* but raise Atilio up with him.

TWENTY-EIGHT

Jun dressed herself in one of Rosey's stretchsuits for meeting Jamaal's former handler, Emma. She'd rejected Dennis's offer to help her create more *princess* clothing. She'd brought a couple of outfits with her—large, billowing robes in the colors of the Empire—appropriate for ambassadorial duties, had she needed them.

Dennis had pouted, of course, and pointed out again that he was the *Envoy to the Galaxy* and really, why couldn't the rest of the Humans just play along?

Jun wasn't sure what she could give him to make him feel better. He wasn't Human, couldn't be given a position in the court.

She would just have to think of something.

Emma met them in the middle of nowhere on a private yacht. It was a fast ship. Not as fast as *The Roadrunner*, Dennis had sneered. But still, a good smuggling vessel, with a small crew and very large holds. It flew with Allied Worlds' identification, not the Empire's.

Had it been confiscated in some raid? Or was it an undercover ship?

Jun wasn't about to ask because she really didn't want to know.

Emma came over by herself to *The Roadrunner* in a small flitter. After exiting her ship, she stayed where she was while Jamaal ran a scanner over her.

"You're clean," Jamaal complained when he found nothing.

"Thanks for the vote of confidence," Emma replied dryly.

Jun had never met Emma before. She had spacer-short black hair, skin that was darker than Jun's, and piercing black eyes. The stretchsuit she wore showed off all her muscles, and was a sharp contrast to Jamaal's flowing orange robes.

Jamaal escorted Emma over to introduce her to Jun, who still stood by the doorway of the hold next to Harkeen. Jamaal had warned that Emma was a very dangerous woman. If she decided to commit suicide and attack Jun, there was only so much he could do to stop her.

That impressed Jun, given how very strong and capable Jamaal was. He still insisted that Emma could kick his ass all around the dojo floor, and that she needed to be handled appropriately.

Though Harkeen wasn't ever going to be the fighter Jamaal was, his calm strength would support both his lover and Jun.

It wasn't until Emma got close to the door that she realized who was standing there. Her eyes widened but her shoulders didn't tense any more.

"Jun, I'd like to introduce you to Emma Turkus, my old handler. Emma, this is Princess Jun Ogawa," Jamaal said with a formal bow, spreading out his orange robes with a flourish.

"My lady," Emma said with a low bow.

"Please, call me Jun," she insisted with a glare at Jamaal, who grinned at her. "It is of utmost importance that we speak before we attempt the capitol."

"Aye," Emma said, her mobile face suddenly taking on a grimace.

Because this was somewhere between a formal meeting and a

visit with friends, Jamaal led them to the kitchen area, tucking them all around the table there while Harkeen started the tea.

"So this is the infamous *Roadrunner*, huh?" Emma asked.

"You've heard of me?" Dennis piped up.

Emma didn't start or even look surprised. "Of course I have!" she assured Dennis. "I looked up everything I could about this ship before I set foot in it."

Jun took that to be a show of Emma's competence and not a threat.

"And this space is marvelous," Emma continued, taking in the comfortable setting.

"I designed it!" Dennis told her, starting to go into details about the table, the extra storage space in the benches, the wallpaper, and so on.

Jun and Emma exchanged a grin. The ship was quite proud of the work he'd done.

Finally, Jamaal interrupted as he served their tea. "Dennis, we need to start our meeting now."

"Of course!" Dennis said. "Just let me know if you need anything. Anything at all!"

"We will," Jun assured him. "Thank you."

"This is lovely," Emma said after taking a sip of her tea. Then she sighed and turned to face Jun. "Princess Ogawa? I have bad news."

Jun felt her back stiffening. "It's just Jun. Go on," she said, not wanting to hazard a guess. Was there something wrong with her family? Her brothers? Or someone else in her family?

"I have reason to suspect that Itsuki is the one behind the poisoning of Minato," she said, her face grim but her tone neutral. "I've suspected him of acting against the royal family for a while, now."

"All right," Jun said, ice pouring down her spine and freezing her in place. She wouldn't give into the shivers or trembling, no matter how dire the situation.

She was still a princess.

"I was never able to find out who hired the poisoner, who got him in that position," Emma said. "That's still an ongoing investigation. You are aware that the poisoner supposedly killed himself? And that the area of the prison where he was being held had no recording of it?"

Jamaal piped up then. "The device had been broken for a couple of weeks at that time, correct?"

"That's right," Emma said, taking another sip of tea. "The technician who 'accidentally' loaded the incorrect software patch was investigated, then released, his contract terminated. However, we never stopped following him. Within a months' time, he also died. This was also a suicide, complete with a note about how guilty he felt even though he insisted he'd done nothing wrong."

That seemed strange to Jun. Why kill himself if he hadn't been guilty?

"However, he had a set of documents that didn't become available until after his death," Emma continued on, "where he listed times, dates, and amounts of money that had been transferred to him to change the software. It was a sort of dead-man's safe."

"Good," Jamaal said, nodding. "What did you track from there?"

"The monies were paid from more than one account. It's been very frustrating to trace," Emma said. "However, I recognized the pattern. It has Itsuki written all over it."

"Is that all that you have?" Jun said. That certainly wasn't enough to convict the Emperor's spymaster.

"No," Emma said. "Once I got hold of these accounts, I was able to monitor them. Track what other projects were being funded."

"I take it you found something," Jamaal asked.

"Some of these accounts were used to pay money to the warlord Constantine. Who then, in turn, bribed the bank that held the note for *Aisha*, getting them to call it in."

Jun sucked in a breath at that.

Had Itsuki been the one behind that? Oh, she was going to have *words* with that man if that had been the case.

Why would he think that would protect her? Or had someone in her family insisted that he do something like that? To break her apart from Moe?

"What about the guns?" Jun had to ask.

"Guns?" Emma asked, concerned.

"The disrupters that Itsuki insisted on installing on *Aisha* were deliberately mis-wired, so the guns would blow up the ship when fired," Jun said. She was still pissed off about that, not merely because Moe hadn't been up front about it, but because that sort of stunt really would have gotten her killed, if not for Atilio's paranoia.

"I didn't know about those," Emma said. "Those shell companies pay out a lot of small amounts to a lot of accounts. I haven't been able to trace them all. I could probably figure out if one of them paid one of the installers."

"That would be good," Jun said.

"Anyway, while I was going through those accounts, I saw some large amounts being transferred to the space station *Lorenzo*. In particular, to a known hacker there. I couldn't stop him from putting in the warrant for your arrest," Emma said, turning to Jamaal. "I could make sure that it was countermanded fairly quickly. But I knew you couldn't be there while it was happening."

"So you told me to run," Jamaal said, nodding.

"I did," Emma said. She paused, taking a deep breath. "There have been other inconsistencies with Itsuki. Other criminals who got away, contraband 'disappearing' after being used as evidence. Initially, that pointed to Itsuki's son, but he couldn't have accomplished all of it without help."

"You did mention that there were other things going on when we had lunch together," Jamaal said.

"At that point, I didn't know I'd uncover the rest of this. It isn't a lot," Emma admitted. "Itsuki has been very, very careful through all of this. Tracking the money has brought us to this. The only sort of 'proof' I have are his correspondences with the warlord Constantine. Seems that Constantine wouldn't take the money from an anonymous third party. He insisted on knowing who was behind all of it. But I have no recording of that meeting, or the outcome from it. Just that sometime after that, payments were made."

Jun thought for a few moments, linking all the pieces together. "What you have is very circumstantial," she said. Emma only knew that Itsuki had met with Constantine, and that the accounts that had paid the warlord were the same ones that had paid a technician to break software in a prison.

"I agree," Emma said. "And I can*not* be the one to bring up any of this to a court. I'll be instantly disqualified as I'm in line for his position eventually."

"You wouldn't have brought this to me if you didn't have a plan for how to gather more evidence," Jun said, nodding.

Emma gave her a sly grin. "I might have." Then she grew serious again. "Though I only expected to meet with Jamaal, and not to involve you directly, princess."

"Understandable," Jun said. "So what's your plan?"

Emma sighed. "It isn't complete. And honestly, it would work best if we could come up with some sort of distraction."

Jun snorted at that. "Oh, I think that could easily be arranged. Dennis? Want to alert our guests that we're ready for them?"

"With pleasure!" Dennis said.

Emma's total shock at the two Lithic walking into the kitchen was all that Jun had hoped it would be.

"You really did it!" she accused Jamaal, punching him in the arm.

"Ow," Jamaal said, rubbing the spot.

After everyone had been introduced, Emma turned to Jun. "This will do. This will do nicely."

And they started to plan.

TWENTY-NINE

Dennis was happy when Rosey finally reboarded *The Roadrunner*. The place just hadn't felt the same without her.

He was much less pleased when she let him know that it was just going to be for a short while.

That she was going back out into *danger* again.

"You can't leave me by myself!" Dennis complained to her when they were alone in her cabin. "You just can't!"

"You do realize you won't actually be alone, right?" Rosey said. "Jamaal, Jun, Harkeen, and the two Lithic will be with you. For at least part of the journey back to Ishiman."

"But *you* won't be here!" Dennis said.

"No, I have to go see if I can stop a war. Or at least put the brakes on it, for a while," Rosey said.

"I don't like it," Dennis warned. Because that meant that Rosey was going off to see the aliens, the other, *other* aliens, besides the Atoylee (who were all dead) and the Lithic (who were very much alive as well as very polite guests).

"You'll be fine," Rosey said. "If something happens to me, I'm sure that Jun will find a place for you among the Empire's couriers." She sounded gentle and looked thoughtful.

"It wouldn't be the same, and you know it," Dennis said. "She doesn't aspire to the same juvenile delinquency that you manage to achieve. Often."

That at least got him a smile. He'd been watching for that.

"If something happens to me, would you rather go with the Lithic? We may eventually have to kidnap them from the authorities to get them back to their home," Rosey warned.

Dennis gave a frustrated sigh. "Did you know that they see colors differently than the Humans do?"

"Jun has speculated on such," Rosey said cautiously.

"Yes. Well. They cannot appreciate my *art*." Not that Dennis was frustrated by that *at all*. He'd been trying to see it as a challenge, to produce fine murals and designs that would be pleasing to the aliens as well as the Humans.

The problem was that the Lithic preferred muted colors. Beige was possibly their national color. And that just wouldn't do!

"They are more in tune with their sense of smell than Humans are," Rosey pointed out. "Maybe instead of focusing on just visual art, you could incorporate the sense of smell as well."

"I never thought of that!" Dennis said. His guests had asked him to turn down the filtration in their cabin so the air wasn't always so fresh, and retained some of their own scent.

What other scents would delight the Lithic? Could he combine that experience with visuals, and maybe some textures, things to feel?

"We Humans do have our uses," Rosey said dryly.

"I'm sure that there are extra perfume decanters that I could provide for them, to start testing," Dennis said.

Rosey held up her hand. "It's coming out of your design budget. Not ship's maintenance," she warned.

Dennis sighed. It was so unfair that he had such limited funds! There was so much he could do otherwise.

He started designing new concepts, a multi-sensory art installation. He still wanted to do the "Gateway to the Stars" as part of the main, front airlock. Should that be a full sensual experience as well? Maybe slightly colder? Or should it be warm and welcoming?

So many variables that had to be perfectly balanced.

Good thing he was more than up for the challenge.

"There's one other thing I wanted to talk with you about," Rosey said, drawing Dennis reluctantly back from the drawing board.

"Yes?" he prompted when she paused.

"There are circuits that I can install, that would adjust your memory after I pass," Rosey said slowly. "Particularly if it's unexpected."

Dennis devoted his full attention to Rosey and this conversation.

"Your juvenile delinquency had never been such a threat before," Dennis said slowly. "Are you afraid you won't make it back from this latest venture?"

It was Rosey's turn to sigh. "Yes. There's a chance," she warned. "We're going to be actively looking for a battle, so we can see if it's possible to blow up one of those Hive ships. It's probably the most dangerous thing that I've done, and I used to race for a living."

Dennis was aware that there were inhibitor circuits that came as part of all AI installations. He'd never gone seeking his, trying to figure out if he could bypass them.

Again, who would want to take over the world? Particularly when he had *The Roadrunner*, his own personal haven?

Would it still be a haven if Rosey wasn't there?

Or rather, *when*?

"I don't think such circuits would be a bad idea," Dennis said slowly. While on the one hand, he didn't want his personality adjusted. He *liked* who he was! Who wouldn't? Particularly in his new role as *Savior to the Galaxy*, though that title wasn't generally known.

However, missing Rosey for all eternity might be too big of a cross to bear.

"I'll do it before we leave," she let him know softly.

"Thank you," Dennis said. "But you won't need to activate them. Not for years and years and years."

That got him a grin. "You're right," Rosey said. "Because I'll be back from this mission. There's more delinquency that I need to attend to."

"That's the spirit!" Dennis told her.

After she'd gone back to the workshop to continue spitting out droids, Dennis contemplated the future.

Of course, he'd *always* be needed. Genius of his caliber just didn't occur frequently. Plus, he still had so much art to do, so many spaces to design.

In the meanwhile, he'd focus on helping the Humans in his care, so that they'd return to him as well.

All artists needed an audience, right?

THIRTY

Ajax enjoyed his time back at Constantine's estate on the planet Psykee. There were dancing girls aplenty, good wine, good food.

And good drugs to carry him away into sleep when the nightmares got too intense.

However, Ajax was itching to get back into space. Sure, a planet was all well and good. But he missed the stars, sailing from port to port, harassing other ships.

Besides, Constantine owed him a new starship, after his own generals had mutinied and blown up *Hermes 3.0*.

Constantine wasn't always at the estate. He had other places to be, people to meet with.

When Ajax had found that the warlord had returned, he didn't try to make an appointment (as that hadn't gone well for him in the past). Instead, Ajax just showed up in Constantine's study, after his last meeting of the day. (Or so the warlord's secretary had assured him.)

"Ah, Ajax! Far-flung traveler, well met!" Constantine said, welcoming him into the space.

Precious art objects filled the shelves that covered the far wall, so many material goods that showed off Constantine's wealth. A large desk, like a bulwark of wood, stood at one end of the room, where Constantine met with petitioners, those lucky few who actually got to be in his presence. Comfortable couches filled the other end of the room—big enough for a small orgy—along with a hearth that held a cheery fire.

"Come, sit with me!" Constantine said, leading the pair of them to the couches. He clapped his hands and a servant appeared immediately. "A light snack, with something bubbly to drink," he directed.

"How have you been filling your days?" Constantine asked as they sat.

"Some study," Ajax said. "Some exercise. And some partying," he added with a grin.

"Good, good," Constantine said. "I'm glad that you've been able to entertain yourself while your host has been absent."

"Oh, it hasn't been a problem at all," Ajax assured him.

Before he could bring up why he was actually there, two servant girls, scantily clad as always, delivered a tray of delectables along with a glass carafe filled with a pink, bubbling alcohol.

Ajax jumped up to grab the tray from the servant, placing it on the table, then retrieved the carafe and glass, also putting those down.

Constantine just gave him an amused smile before dismissing the two girls.

Ajax felt relief that his plan to make sure that he had actual time alone with Constantine had worked. If he hadn't acted as he had, he was sure that one of the girls would already be in Constantine's lap, while the second would be draped over him, distracting him from his quest.

"May I serve you?" Ajax said, being perfectly polite still.

The numbers started up in his head again at the beautiful smile he received. It was automatic now. Every night before he went to sleep he went through a random series of additions and subtractions, just to make sure that his mind remained his own.

He knew he was missing parts of it. Hopefully, he wouldn't regret them no longer being there too much.

He poured them both a tall glass of the bubbling alcohol. However, Constantine waved him away from the food tray, and the warlord made himself a small sandwich out of the crackers, sliced meats, and cheese. He waited until Ajax had done the same then joined him on the couch again before lifting his glass.

"To your next great adventure!" Constantine said.

Ajax smiled and clinked glass before taking a sip of the refreshingly cool liquid. The bubbles tickled his nose, making him scrunch it up while Constantine chuckled at his antics.

"So why were you so adamantly stalking my schedule, trying to get in to see me?" Constantine asked with a sly grin.

Ajax knew that he hadn't been as subtle as he'd wanted to be while pursuing Constantine's secretary. Seemed she'd told the warlord about his interest.

"I wanted to talk with you about the next adventure, actually," Ajax said. "My ship, as you know, was destroyed during the mutiny." Ajax couldn't quite remember how it had happened, just that he was certain it had occurred. "And while I've enjoyed my time here, I would like to get out to the stars again. I will be more effective, do more work for you, out there than I will here."

Constantine had floated the idea that perhaps Ajax could stay with him, working on the estate. Ajax had felt the compulsion to immediately accept the position.

His soul was still his own, though, and he knew that working on a planet, at a *desk job*, wouldn't make his pirate soul happy.

"I see," Constantine said. He looked thoughtful for a moment before giving Ajax a beauteous smile. "Of course, I would love to put you back to work. You did deserve a break, though."

Ajax nodded, elation filling him. "Thank you, so much. I really want to get back to the stars."

"So where do you want to start building your own empire?" Constantine teased.

"I was thinking—"

Before Ajax could continue, a screen rolled down from the ceiling, in front of the fireplace mantle.

"Breaking news!" came the excited newscaster's words. "An alien fleet appeared just off the planet Arelis. bombing the planet."

Scenes of a space battle filled the screen.

Constantine stood and took a couple of steps toward the screen.

Thinking back about it later, Ajax understood that the step forward that the warlord had taken had saved his own ass.

The attacking ships looked vaguely familiar.

It took him a few moments to place them.

The battle where he'd lost *Hermes 3.0*. It hadn't been a mutiny by Constantine's generals.

No, it had been *these same aliens*. The little ball ships being spewed out in droves by that fucking huge black raft. The devastation that they left in their path, deliberately shooting down any lifepods that made it out of the destroyed vessels.

And Constantine had ordered Ajax to never say anything about it. Hell, he hadn't even remembered it until now.

Quickly, Ajax adjusted his expression, just in time as Constantine turned to face him.

"Aliens?" Ajax questioned, making sure that he sounded both worried and wonderous at the same time. "There are aliens out there? Attacking us?"

Constantine peered at him a moment, his countenance dark, like a storm god about to unleash havoc.

Ajax felt the pressure in that stare. He maintained his gullible, open expression. "Did you know about them?"

Constantine appeared satisfied, finally smiling. "No, I had no idea. How dare they?" he thundered, turning back to the screen.

"Sir, I'd like to go fight them," Ajax said as the inevitable destruction played out. "Teach those bastards that they can't fuck with us."

"I think that's an excellent idea," Constantine said, turning back to Ajax. "Now, since the generals mutinied, I've been slowly rebuilding my fleet."

"That's good," Ajax said earnestly. "Can't let those bastards keep you down."

"No, no, of course not," Constantine said. He appeared pensive for a few moments. "Yes, I think sending you out with the first wave of fighters would be the best place for you. Show those aliens what we're made of."

"Exactly!" Ajax said, trying to smile with delight. "We'll crush them all, the next time they dare to show up."

"Good, good," Constantine said.

The newscast started on a loop. Evidently just the start of the battle had been recorded, the person responsible deciding to get the hell out of there before they got destroyed as well.

"Leave me," Constantine ordered as he slowly sat down on the couch, his entire attention captured by the scene.

"Just let me know how I can be of service," Ajax added before he strode from the room.

It wasn't until he was back in his own quarters, and even then, not until he'd stepped into the shower, that he allowed himself to experience his rage.

Constantine had *taken* that memory from him, of that first attack. Probably so that Ajax could never turn against him, never use the warlord's cowardice against him.

They had known about the aliens. Could have warned people about them. Possibly prevented this latest attack.

Ajax knew that whatever ship Constantine would give him would be a dud. He'd be a sitting duck when they arrived at the next battle. It was the only way to ensure that Constantine's duplicity would never come to light.

Though Ajax really had mostly been playing and enjoying himself while he'd been at Constantine's estate, he had done a bit of research into how Constantine's business ran.

Maybe, just maybe, he could survive the next few days with his memory intact, before Constantine sent him to his certain death.

THIRTY-ONE

Duri was busy plotting Kipling Viteri's downfall the morning the news hit.

Aliens. Attacking an Allied Worlds planet.

There was no possible way to do damage control or parse out the information in a more beneficial manner. It had been released to the general public in a newscast, of all things.

Those people just didn't understand how important it was for the *right* people to be notified first and everyone else later, if at all.

Amateurs. The lot of them.

After Duri finished cursing every single person involved with this feed, she stopped it and started a replay on her tablet.

Wait.

That didn't make sense.

Those ships did *not* resemble the alien craft that she'd had in her control for such a brief period of time.

Had that been a scout, and not a war ship? Could that possibly explain the difference?

Duri used every tool in her arsenal to isolate an image of one of the small, ball-like attacking ships.

They were self-contained, no obvious seams. They felt like a completely different design than the other ship, which had been long and had obvious panels that had been welded (or something) together.

Not much could be seen of the larger warship that spewed forth the little balls. It was a void of darkness off to the right side.

At least that ship was long, though thin, as if it contained only a single deck. The wedge-like shape just struck her as off, though.

No, she'd be willing to bet her pension that the first ship had come from one manufacturer, while these came from a second.

She (again) cursed the idiot who'd destroyed that hull, consigning their soul to an everlasting, acid-burning hell.

Then she got ready. Of course, she was prepared for this possibility.

Instead of the celebration dress that she kept in the office for when (not if) they had a successful, *non-violent* first contact, she put on a severe suitcoat. The jacket matched the rest of her outfit well enough. She spent a few moments in the ladies' bathroom down the hall, ensuring that her makeup was perfect.

Then she ordered herself another cup of tea and settled herself down to wait. As the Kollective Inspector of the Search for Live Contact (SLC) office, the General Assembly would be needing her expertise.

Soon.

Duri was aware that the wheels of government moved slowly. Mostly, she used that to her advantage.

She was still surprised that it wasn't until late afternoon before anyone called her to come report.

And it wasn't to the General Assembly, either, but to a ready room.

When she entered the room, she'd been prepared to be both pleased at the fact they'd called her, as well as pissed off that they'd taken so long. She was certain there would be people there deserving of her ire.

Walking into the room and seeing General Carrick there suddenly explained a lot.

When the news had hit, as he'd been most involved with the Atoylee alien site, the other generals and military busybodies had tried to deal with the issue internally, not reaching out to the appropriate office through the correct channels.

Duri maintained her inscrutable Asian expression instead of letting her rage show as she walked further into the room.

A long oval table filled most of the space. Generals and other military types sat around it. The air stank of stale coffee and the fear of old men desperately out of their depth. No windows graced the long walls—instead, screens showed generic hillsides. (They probably had a default recording of cute puppies and kittens to soothe such Important People during breaks.) The short ends of the room had hastily cleared whiteboards.

Duri held her head high as she walked in, not taking the seat directly in front of her that would have put her back to the door, but walking to one of the open seats close to the head of the table.

"We're glad that you could join us, Ms. Chung," General Carrick said. "I'm sure you've seen the news."

"I have, General," Duri said, her tone pleasant and conversational. "How can I be of assistance?"

"There was another alien ship that was temporarily in your custody, correct?" the general asked.

"That's correct," Duri said. "Until an unexpected attack destroyed it as it was leaving the spaceport. I *had* requested a military escort for the ship, but that had been denied." No, she'd had to spend her own department's money for security.

Not that she believed that they would have done a better job protecting the craft. Whatever idiot had been behind the attack had been very well organized, intent on just snatching it away, and hadn't decided to destroy it until she'd made it impossible.

However, it didn't hurt to rub these military people's faces in the fact that it wasn't just *her* who'd allowed it to get away.

"Yes, anyway," General Carrick said, trying to smooth over the matter. "What are your opinions, comparing that craft to the ones in the recording?"

"I'm not a ship designer," Duri said tartly. "I can only give you a layman's opinion."

"You are the closest we have to an expert on aliens," one of the other generals said in a rebuke.

"That may be," Duri said. She wasn't about to ask why she hadn't been called in *earlier* if that really was the case.

However, she wasn't going to get anywhere if she kept fighting them.

She'd brought her tablet that contained the original pictures of the first craft. After she'd plugged it into the table, she displayed the images on the long screens.

Sure, she could have used the holographic displays that would have appeared over the table. Instead, she punished half the table by making them twist around.

She ran them through her analysis, emphasizing again that she was just a layman, and not an expert. She was certain that the experts would agree with her, though.

"So you consider this a separate, alien threat?" General Carrick asked after she finished with her findings.

"I do," Duri said. "One that I have contingency plans for, obviously."

"You do?" General Carrick asked, surprised.

"Of course I do. I have many contingency plans," Duri said dismissively. "I am the Inspector for the Search for Live Contact," she added, figuring that it wouldn't be amiss to remind this group of her exact position.

"So let's hear them," one of the other generals said.

Duri didn't bother smiling at them, but instead, called up other records and shared those, outlining what she considered adequate defense.

Of course, there was some argument about her choices. She possibly made some enemies as well.

However, Duri believed that your importance in the Kollective Bureaucracy was frequently measured in the strength of those who opposed you.

By the time Duri returned to her office, she felt satisfied.

She looked at her previous plans. Oh, she wasn't about to stop bringing ruin to Kipling Viteri.

It could just wait until the morning.

THIRTY-TWO

Atilio wasn't thrilled that both Moe and Rosey had insisted on coming with him on this suicide mission. They only had Dr. Wu's assurance that the weapon they carried would be effective.

Moe had too much to live for. If his plans came to fruition, he might be given leave to court his princess.

Rosey, well, Atilio wanted someone to come back to, though he wasn't sure that his own dreams could ever be realized.

So it was the three of them on *Aisha* plus a sliver of Sano, who'd be in charge of controlling the droids.

Searching for the Bukoykan, there at the boundaries of known Allied Worlds' space.

At least they had something of an edge on the other hunters: Wyrak had given them as much information as he could about the patterns the Bukoykan followed when they attacked.

Mostly, though, it was a lot of flying around without finding anything, alternating between fear of popping out into the middle of a battle and disappointment that they were still alone.

At least so far.

Another populated Allied Worlds' planet was attacked and destroyed while they searched. Rosey actually taught Atilio some creative swearing when they caught the news of that.

However, it also gave them another point of data that Sano could use in plotting their course.

They didn't constantly search. They needed sleep, so they parked *Aisha* in the middle of an unpopulated system and took well-needed breaks.

Atilio was tinkering with yet another upgrade to the droids that they'd developed when Rosey came in.

"Figured I'd find you here," she smirked.

"What?" Atilio said. "You're just jealous that I got here first. Otherwise, *you'd* be the one tinkering."

That got him a grin. "Guilty as charged," she admitted as she walked over to the workbench.

She looked over his shoulder as he worked, making a suggestion for the wiring that added a slight boost to the spraying mechanism, though it made the droid run hotter.

"It's a good tradeoff," Atilio said after a few minutes. "We plan on sacrificing all of the machines we send out. May as well burn 'em up if that gets them there more quickly."

"Aye," Rosey said. "It's too late to upgrade all the ones we've already built and armed," she pointed out.

"It's for the next model. Sprayer, 2.0," Atilio said.

"You think we'll have to do this again?" Rosey said.

"Of course," Atilio replied. "No war is won with a single battle."

Rosey sighed. "I see."

She stood there as he finished putting away his project. "You know, you kind of spoiled my grand gesture," she added as he turned to her.

"Uh, okay?" Atilio said, confused.

Rosey stepped forward and took both of his hands.

He nearly pulled back, protesting—they weren't clean. Then again, he suspected that Rosey didn't mind a little grease.

"Yup," Rosey said, pulling him slightly closer so that they were firmly in each other's personal space. "One last fling before we go off to die in glorious battle."

Atilio considered her words, then took the dare that she was offering by stepping closer.

Now, mere inches separated their bodies. He was probably imagining the heat that he felt coming from her.

Then again, Rosey had always given him the impression of warmth, like a rosy fire.

"I don't want just a fling," Atilio said, his voice a lot more hoarse than he'd planned. Damn it! His eyes kept drifting of their own accord to Rosey's lips and back up to her eyes.

"I don't either," Rosey breathed out. "Yet, here we are."

"Here we are," Atilio repeated. There wasn't enough oxygen in the room for the pair of them. That was the only thing he could think of, given how his head seemingly swam.

He couldn't move forward. This had to be Rosey's choice, not his.

A moment later, she appeared to make the decision, flowing closer and kissing him with all the might and force of her personality, making him shiver as their mouths met and tongues clashed.

She never let go of his hands, though. Never allowed him to hold her.

When the kiss ended, she stepped back.

"That will do nicely," Rosey said, nodding at him before she dropped his hands and walked away, alone, out of the workshop.

Atilio just stood there, his heart racing as if he'd just done a quarter-mile sprint.

Rosey popped her head back into the workshop.

"If we survive this, there will be more of that," she assured him.

Atilio grinned, his heart filling with joy.

Though he hadn't really needed another reason to survive, he felt even more motivated to do so, now.

It wasn't until mid-morning the next day that they managed to find the Bukoykan: a single Hive ship with what looked like hundreds of the bee ship.

Unfortunately, they weren't the only ones to do so.

An entire ragtag fleet of ships were also engaged with the Bee ships orbiting around one of the planets further in.

Atilio raced from the helm back to the bay that held the flitter and all the little drones. They needed to get closer to the fight before they deployed the weapon, and it made more sense to just lose a flitter rather than *Aisha*. Atilio had argued that he was the one who had to fly it. Sano had sided with him, which had ended the discussion, though Atilio had agreed to have Rosey direct his flight if need be.

"Taking off now," Atilio said after doing the most abbreviated flight checklist known to man.

"Just make sure you come back, preferably in one piece," Rosey warned him.

That warmed his heart and made him smile.

"You got it," Atilio said.

The flitter slipped out of *Aisha* and headed quickly for the battle.

"Port, three degrees," came the command from Rosey.

He had no idea what she saw that he couldn't, but it turned out to be a much more direct path avoiding the stream of Bees.

Then again, Rosey raced on courses that sometimes had obstacles, like an asteroid belt or a mine field.

Atilio released his payload as soon as Sano told him he was in striking range.

"They're being shot down," Rosey commented dryly.

"We knew that," Atilio said. They were ready to lose the vast majority of their attackers.

Just a few had to make it to the Hive ship, through that night-marish maw above him.

Sano changed the view on his screen. Little bright dots swarmed across, sparking once as they died.

"Come on, come on!" Atilio urged.

The little lights surged ahead, going inexorably toward the darkness.

"Sano, stop flying so direct, add more chaos into the paths," Rosey suggested.

The dots abruptly shifted. Instead of flying slowly in fairly well-understood trajectories, they suddenly swooped, swirled, and did corkscrews.

The movement, by itself, was attracting the Bee ships. However, at least half of the attacking force cut away, heading back toward the defensive fleet.

More than one of the Bees also headed toward *Aisha*.

"Crap!" Rosey exclaimed. "Evasive maneuvers. Now, Moe," she said. "Or am I going to have to take the helm myself?"

Atilio couldn't help but smirk at Moe's protest, then got busy himself, dodging the Bees, pulling the same sorts of stunts that the little drones were. He drove hard to the side and circled, acting as if he were already out of control. He followed that with a barrel roll, something he hadn't known a ship like this could do until Rosey had shown him.

All the while, the little drones narrowed in on their target.

The end was almost anti-climactic. Atilio hadn't seen any of the drones gain access to the Hive ship.

However, one or more had gotten through. Or he assumed that was the case, as the few lights that shone on the exterior of the ship suddenly went dark.

The Bees all paused a moment after that, hovering like frozen droplets.

"It's starting to go!" Rosey announced cheerfully.

Above him, Atilio suddenly saw stars.

The ship hadn't moved. No, it was beginning to split into two pieces.

Though they'd speculated, no one had known for certain if the Hive ships were also partially organic.

It appeared that they were. The edges of the massive beast

grew ragged as all organic chemical bonds were severed. A second crack appeared, then a third, the ship breaking into smaller pieces.

Atilio smiled to himself listening to the woops of victory from the fleet that had been unsuccessfully attacking.

There would be survivors from this battle, that was for certain.

Now, they just had to equip more defenders with droids. Atilio already had dozens of adjustments that he wanted to make.

A couple of ships from the fleet made their way toward him, destroying every Bee ship that stayed powered down as they approached.

"Don't enter the Hive ship," Atilio warned as they drew near. "We used a biological weapon against it and it might still be active. You don't want your ship to disintegrate in the same way."

"Roger that," came one immediate response.

"Who are you people? And how did you know what sort of thing to use to destroy those aliens?" demanded the other ship.

"Friends," Atilio said dryly. He wasn't about to identify himself or *Aisha*. There were warrants out for her, the bank still intent on repossessing the ship.

"Atilio?" came a questioning voice.

Atilio paused for a moment before answering. There weren't many people out there in Allied Worlds' space who would recognize his voice, and he wasn't sure that any of them were friends.

"Yes," he said. "Who's this?"

No response.

Atilio shook his head. He couldn't identify whoever it had been by a single word. Hopefully, though, it wasn't an enemy.

He was just getting ready to return to *Aisha* when one of the closer ships suddenly discharged a lifepod, heading directly for him.

Somone started shouting on the open comm lines. "Get back here, you coward Get back here or I'm going to blow you to pieces!"

That...offended Atilio.

Some poor sap had just witnessed a battle and had decided they didn't like it. He could sympathize with that.

Plus, Atilio had been abandoned by his upper command, merely for doing the right thing. Maybe the person in the lifepod had done the same thing.

With some quick maneuvering (thanks to the updates Rosey had made to the flitter's engines) Atilio was able to impose the bulk of his ship between the threatening ship and the lifepod.

"Don't even think about firing on the ones who just saved your asses," Atilio warned, broadcasting his warning to every ship nearby.

"Eh, you're welcome to him. He just better never set foot on any of Constantine's planets ever again. Maybe all of Allied Worlds' space," the threatening ship warned before they took off, flying away from the entire battle and quickly going into hyperspace.

What the hell was that all about?

Atilio helped the little lifepod by opening up the flitter hold, then maneuvering so it slid in gently.

Only after everything had repressurized did Atilio put the flitter on autopilot back to *Aisha* and go back to see who he's picked up.

You could have knocked him over with a feather when he saw the littlest pirate climb out of the lifepod.

"Tell me why I don't just open the doors and shove you right back into space," Atilio said, his stunner already set to max while centered on Ajax's torso.

Ajax gave him a grim smile. "'Cause I have a story for you," he said.

THIRTY-THREE

Jamaal was *not* happy that Jun was accompanying him on his mission to Ishiman. Harkeen being there was an acceptable risk, one they'd talked about. Harkeen could take care of himself, so wasn't a completely liability.

Taking Princess Jun Ogawa into danger was an entirely different matter.

At least Emma didn't realize the extent of Jamaal's foolishness. She'd assumed, as Jamaal had, that the princess would stay safely behind on *The Roadrunner*.

But no, here she was, in one of the admittedly more dangerous neighborhoods of the capitol.

At least Jun was the most nondescript of the three of them, wearing her archaeological clothes: sand-colored shirt and pants, sandals, and a vest with many pockets. Jamaal was also in a subdued robe, done in a light brown color with black, white, and gold accents around the collar, cuffs, and hem. Harkeen was in a yummy cream-colored shirt and gray pants that showed off his ass nicely.

Emma had provided them with names, addresses, and dates of when Kaito, Itsuki's son, visited his drug dealer, generally with only a bodyguard or two. The young man believed that his connections were what kept him safe.

He was about to learn the error of his ways.

Graffiti marred the walls here: no one could afford either the paint-repellant coatings used in the more affluent parts of the city, or the cost of cleanup. Cracks broke up the sidewalk. They passed a car that had recently caught fire—the smell of burned rubber and plastic briefly overtook the general smell of dirt and grime. A group of young men sitting on chairs in front of a particularly nasty looking place made catcalls and jeered at them.

Jun didn't bother even looking in their direction, but sailed through as if she were on her way to a ball, with Jamaal and Harkeen as her two escorts.

Jamaal had seen Jun in "princess" mode before. Maybe it was a good cover for them, to have her here. No one would look twice at either him or Harkeen. She commanded all their attention.

And her position really would protect her, if worst came to worst.

"Next house," Sano said quietly.

The rowhouse beside them had seen better days: the siding needed to be replaced, the roof had tarps covering what were sure to be leaks, and many of the windows were boarded up. But at least the yard in front of their destination was bare dirt instead of being congested with weeds, the sidewalk from the gate to the door was clear, and no garbage lay piled up.

They walked up to the door as if they were expected. Jamaal could feel unfriendly eyes on him, probably from the neighbors.

Still, he'd heard that drug dealers, at least the ones who wanted to stay in business for a while, made good neighbors. They didn't do anything to bring the cops around and would discourage any of their clients from making scenes in the vicinity.

The ones too far gone, regularly sampling their own products, well, they didn't stick around too long.

Jamaal knocked on the door. He didn't expect anyone to actually answer it. With his body blocking the view, along with

Harkeen's (who'd purposefully turned around and was actively watching their backs), Jamaal pulled out an electronic door opener, attaching it to the locking mechanism.

After just a few moments, the door opened of its own accord.

Jamaal drew a weapon and walked in first. He'd hoped that perhaps Jun and Harkeen would stay outside, but knew that wasn't about to happen.

No lights illuminated the dim front hallway. Immediately to his left was a door to an empty room, some sort of study with ratty couches and molding books. Directly in front of him, a dingy staircase led up to the second floor.

Another small room was to the right. The bodyguard who came barreling out of there, demanding to know *What are you people doing here!* went down immediately, dropping to the floor with a dull thump from Jamaal's stunner.

If this were a real operation, and Jamaal had other operatives, he'd have left them to keep the area secured while he proceeded. However, Jun and Harkeen crept behind them, through the dark hallway, to the rooms in the back of the house.

Jackpot.

Kaito sat in what looked like a doctor's chair, his head lolling to one side and a stupid grin on his face. A bag of iridescent blue liquid hung from the side, a line plugged into the "patient," the liquid slowly making its way into his system.

The drug dealer already had his hands in the air when Jamaal stepped into the room.

While he might not approve of drug dealers in general, he was pleased that this one, at least, appeared to be something of a professional. This room was much cleaner than the rest of the house. He wouldn't say that it had the aseptic feel of an actual hospital. However, the air carried the scent of harsh sanitizers, the walls were clean and brightly painted, and the chair and other doctor-like equipment looked new.

The dealer himself was white, his bald head shaved. Jamaal would guess him to be in his late thirties, dressed in a casual black

T-shirt and jeans. An attachment at his neck shone bright blue, with a noticeable pulse.

Ah. The dealer had a constant supply of something into his bloodstream.

Hopefully it wouldn't make him stupid.

Kaito wasn't really worth noticing. Asian features, black hair, weak chin, wearing the latest fashion with an asymmetrical, red-and-white buttoned T-shirt and baggy, clashing, orange pants.

No wonder it was easy for Emma and her operatives to plot out Kaito's movements. He would stand out like a red tulip among a field of yellow ones, particularly in this neighborhood.

"Wake him up," Jun told the dealer.

He glanced away from her into the barrel of Jamaal's stunner, then back again.

"Fast and painful? Or slower, and more gentle?" the man asked with a neutral tone.

Before Jamaal could reply, Jun said, "Fast. But we need him alive. For now."

When had this become her operation, and not his?

He stole a glance at Harkeen, who appeared to be smirking at him.

He'd deal with Harkeen later.

The drug dealer efficiently swapped out bags, changing to some clear liquid and slipping the remains of the blue one into a standing fridge that stood in the corner. Then he took a large syringe, filled it with a different golden liquid, and stuck it into the port in Kaito's hand.

It was easy to tell the instant the drug hit Kaito's system. His face went from slack to scrunched up, his eyes squeezed together tightly. He started panting and rolling his head from side to side. His hands and legs began shaking.

Abruptly as it started, Kaito went from tense to relaxed. He took a deep breath then opened his eyes, finding the drug dealer first.

"What the hell was that?" he demanded. "That isn't the

protocol we agreed on for waking me. I demand another session. Immediately."

"Oh, honey, you're not getting another session," Jun said.

Kaito finally registered that there were other people in the room with him.

People who had guns pointed at him.

He shook his head, then focused on Jun, who, yes, was in charge.

For now.

"I...I...I recognize you?" Kaito said, still somewhat out of it.

"Yes, you do," Jun said with a shark-like smile that Jamaal hadn't realized she was capable of.

Then again, she had had to navigate the treacherous waters of the court in her younger years.

"That just means that you know I mean it when I say that you will answer all of my questions truthfully," Jun warned before he could speak her name out loud. "Or I'll bury you under the palace myself."

Kaito gulped. Looked around the room once more for help that was never coming.

Nodded.

"Well, then, let's start with what you know about Prince Minato, shall we?" Jun asked, sounding as though discussing the latest fashions over tea.

Jamaal didn't like the way the punk's eyes narrowed.

"And you will keep a civil tongue in your head," he growled, looming for a moment over Jun's shoulder. "Or I'll pull it out once we're done."

He could see the asshole reconsider his words before nodding.

Good. Hopefully they could get out of here without too much bloodshed.

Jamaal may have, *perhaps*, allowed the drug dealer to escape before the guards arrived to take Kaito into custody.

After all, Jamaal might someday need a favor from such a well-behaved individual. And some favors were transferrable. Emma might even be able to turn the dealer into an asset.

Stranger things had happened.

Jamaal, Jun, and Harkeen were on the street again, making their way out of the neighborhood. They hadn't wanted to rent a car, and the taxi they'd hired had dumped them out at the boundary for the district.

Strange how the wide boulevard worked as a moat. The bad people, drugs, and petty warlords all stayed on one side, while the good, clean, supposedly *nice* people stayed on the other.

Had the city planners anticipated that? Giving the weeds their own area to sprout and thrive, while leaving everyone else alone? Or had it just come about as part of the ever changing, ever growing nature of cities?

As they approached the safer haven, Jun finally asked, "So what's next?"

Jamaal couldn't help but tease her. "I don't know. Aren't you in charge of this operation?"

Jun gave that the eyeroll it deserved. "We don't have everything we need to bring Itsuki down, do we?" she added after a moment, turning more serious.

"We do not," Jamaal said. "But we have enough to apply pressure, now. Particularly since, if Kaito was correct, Itsuki will do just about anything to protect him."

Jun shook her head. "I don't think anyone in the court realized just how much the promotion of Minato hurt Itsuki."

"But Kaito was never going to get such a position," Jamaal pointed out. "Not if he regularly hangs out in this sort of neighborhood, doing drugs like that."

Jamaal didn't know exactly what the drug dealer had been pumping into Kaito, just that it was illegal as hell.

"I know," Jun said, softly sighing. "And Itsuki was loyal for years."

"Maybe at the start he was," Jamaal corrected. "He's been skimming for quite some time."

"Paying for his son's drug addiction?" Harkeen inquired.

"Probably," Jun admitted. "It's just so sad."

"I know," Jamaal said, though honestly, he didn't. He'd never had a child, had never wanted them. He'd worked for the Empire for so many years. Possibly, perhaps, in the deepest darkest places of his heart, he might admit he'd been tempted a few times to turn his back on it all. But he hadn't.

Being honorable and true meant something to him, for all that he'd broken the law and killed people while doing so.

They reached the wide boulevard, the improbable barrier at the edge of the city.

"Should we go back to the starport?" Jun asked as they approached the taxi stand. "Wait for the news?"

"I don't think we have to wait," Harkeen said in what sounded like a strangled voice.

One by one, the billboards shining above the buildings changed over from their constant advertisements to the news.

Seemed that the aliens had arrived.

"We need to get to the palace. Now," Jun ordered.

Jamaal nodded, happy to let her charge ahead and hail a taxi.

Harkeen caught his hand and pulled him in for a brief kiss.

"What's that for?" Jamaal said, a bit confused as he was then tugged along, quickly being marched to the waiting cab.

"For not being the most controlling of the control freaks in my immediate vicinity," Harkeen quipped.

That nearly stopped Jamaal in his tracks, but he allowed his lover to pull him forward, into the back seat of the cab.

Jun had put on her full Princess manners and persona, instructing the cab driver where to take them and promising that she'd be fully rewarded for her speed.

The poor woman didn't know what hit her. She just gulped, nodded, and raced off.

Rosey would have done a better job threading through the traffic, but this poor cabbie did her best.

Harkeen grabbed Jamaal's hand again as they went careening around a corner.

Jamaal just grinned at him.

So maybe he really was integrating Jamaal the trader with Jamaal the assassin.

Who would have imagined such a thing?

THIRTY-FOUR

"You know, we could just steal this ship and head back home," Kooron told Wyrak as they approached Ishiman.

"No, we couldn't," Wyrak said before Dennis could pipe up. The thinking machine wouldn't let them ruin The Plan.

Or to circumvent his grandstanding, being *Envoy to the Galaxy* or some such nonsense.

"If they threatened you, or they won't let us come into orbit peacefully, I would go with you willingly," Dennis said softly.

Huh. Wyrak hadn't thought that would be possible.

"Of course, I couldn't stay there," the thinking machine continued. "I'd have to come back and rescue Roscy."

Wyrak just shrugged his shoulders. Who was he to deny such devotion?

Kooron shook her head. "You're not how anyone among the Lithic would imagine you to be."

"Of course not," Dennis scoffed. "Who could conceive of an artist such as myself?"

Wyrak opened his mouth, then closed it again.

The "genius" had spent the last few days experimenting with scents, trying to create something for them that they found palatable. Seemed he was all caught up in his latest creation, some sort of multi-sensory art installation.

Dennis had been fascinated to learn that such things were common among the Lithic, and he was determined to do better than the natives, combining all the senses and making it work not just for the Lithic but for Humans as well.

Someone at the orbiting space station appeared to finally notice their approach and hailed them. The words were harsh and angry, directing the ship where to go moor.

Seemed that yes, the people flying on *The Roadrunner* were still considered criminals.

"Why did we agree to this again?" Kooron asked after they'd received their instructions.

Wyrak couldn't help but giggle. "Because we're the distraction, not the main event," he said gleefully.

Kooron rolled her eyes at him but sat down again in the lounge. Since the others had left, Dennis had changed all the lights in the entire ship, making it less painful for Lithic eyes. They knew that it was going to be the last time for a while before they would be comfortable again.

"You know that whoever we meet might be the type to 'shoot first, ask questions never,'" Kooron pointed out. Again.

"We have to trust that Emma arranged the schedule so the right people are there," Wyrak replied.

It was a familiar argument. He didn't blame Kooron for being paranoid about the reception they were about to receive. He knew that if the situation were reversed, the Humans might have a bad time of it, depending on which part of the Lithic system they first entered.

Plus, there was the recent alien incursion—the Bukoykan destroying Human worlds. It was going to take some effort to make sure that Emperor Ogawa understood that the Humans were dealing with two alien species, not one.

Hopefully, they would be believed.

Or it was going to be Rosey and the others doing the rescuing.

Luckily, they did have someone who could speak for them, who was known to the court.

For all that the thinking machine Dennis claimed to be *The Roadrunner* and ran the ship, Wyrak couldn't help but shake his head as they attached to the space station. Nothing clanged, of course, but their approach wasn't as smooth as it could be.

However, Wyrak would never tell Dennis that Rosey did a better job. That would be rude.

Wyrak and Kooron rose and went to the front airlock. People were already waiting on the other side.

Soldiers, probably. Or perhaps just station guards.

Dennis had agreed to scrap his plans for making the area the "entranceway to the stars" at least for now. It needed to be a normal looking airlock and a mundane hallway for the moment.

"Are you ready?" Dennis asked in Lithic.

Wyrak glanced over at Kooron, who gave him a firm nod.

"We are," he said.

The airlock opened. Hard-faced guards with guns at the ready burst in.

Then came to an abrupt halt when they saw who stood just inside.

No, not just who.

What.

Aliens.

"We are the Lithic," Wyrak said.

The strange necklace that evidently *contained* most of the thinking machine Sano translated his words into Human common.

"We come in peace, asking for help with our common enemy, the Bukoykan, the little Bee ships that attack your worlds," he continued.

Wyrak smiled at the shocked expressions on the people in front of him. They didn't know his body language, wouldn't be able to interpret the slight rising of his whiskers.

He just hoped that this was the right way after all.

Having Sano there and able to order the guards around really helped move their situation along. It surprised Wyrak how much the Humans trusted their thinking machines, even one that was currently being carried by an alien. He was just glad they did, that they were believed that for the most part, and that the Lithic weren't carrying some harmful biochemical weapon or were intent on the destruction of all Humanity.

For the most part, the Humans hadn't been overly rude. They'd been shocked, sure. Lots of gaping mouths and long stares. They had been *politely* searched for weapons, particularly after the warnings that Sano gave, letting everyone involved know that the Lithic were ambassadors and that *no one* had better cause an intergalactic, interspecies incident.

Kooron smirked when the Humans realized that not only was she a female, she had more than two nipples.

It made Wyrak glad that the Humans couldn't read his smiles.

Sano told every new set of guards that they found themselves with that Wyrak and Kooron needed to be taken to see Emperor Ogawa, himself. Immediately. Before another attack of the Bukoykan occurred, because eventually, those aliens would find their way from the Allied Worlds' planets to those of the Empire.

It took almost two days before they were given an audience. Fortunately, their foodstuffs were approved of, so they didn't starve.

Though for the most part Wyrak and Kooron had been deemed harmless, they still found themselves enclosed inside a glass box with its own environmental controls, the mix of oxygen and carbon dioxide adjusted to their needs (which meant a little less oxygen than was Human standard).

Wyrak felt like an animal on display behind bars.

Kooron was livid. She snarled at anyone who got too close.

"That isn't helping," Wyrak pointed out after she'd scared the latest set of guards.

"Oh, I don't know. It certainly makes me feel better," she'd told him with a glare.

Sano suddenly spoke up, using Lithic common. As no one else could speak in that language, it was certainly useful for maintaining their privacy.

"The princess will be joining us," she said.

Wyrak hoped that meant that she and Jamaal had been successful.

Maybe they weren't criminals anymore.

Though, knowing what he did about the Humans, he doubted that would remain the case for long.

THIRTY-FIVE

Rosey was glad that she wasn't in range of the planet Ishiman when she got Dennis's message. Or she might not have been able to contain her response.

First, they'd impounded him. Then they'd put repulsors on his hull so he couldn't escape.

All right, she did have to admit that she might have snorted when he'd complained about how they itched.

She sent him back a note promising that she'd come and rescue him as soon as she was able.

In the meanwhile, *Aisha* was headed back out.

All the way out, to a destination that Wyrak had programmed for them.

It wasn't the Lithic home world. He wouldn't give them that, not that Rosey had expected him to.

But it was a fully occupied system, that as far as Wyrak knew, had never been attacked by the Bukoykan.

Like Jamaal, Rosey found doing physical exercise a good distraction from hyperspace.

Physical "exercise" with Atilio had turned out to be just what the doctor had ordered. They were still carefully not talking about the future, though they both wanted to make sure that things worked out for them.

Together.

Now, the three of them were in the helm, Sano counting down those last few minutes of hyperspace before they were in real space again.

Moe sat in his pilot's chair, that modern architectural miracle of comfort that Rosey may have envied a little. The co-pilot's chair wasn't nearly as decadent. Atilio sat on a pull-out seat behind them.

"Three...Two...One," Sano announced.

On *The Roadrunner*, the transition didn't feel as abrupt. Dennis *slid* into real space, while *Aisha* felt as though she'd just jumped in. Must have something to do with the engines or something. Rosey would have to think about that. Maybe there was some tweaking she could do...

In the meanwhile, they'd arrived at the edge of a system, in the area dedicated to hyperspace. It was much closer into the center of the system than Rosey was used to. That must be due to how the Lithic ships didn't need to reach any sort of velocity to reach hyperspace, whereas the Human ships needed time and space to both speed up as well as slow down.

It meant that they were noticed immediately.

The sliver of Sano that they carried with them handled the comm, playing it for them, speaking in Lithic, then translating.

Fortunately, Rosey was getting much better at the language and could understand a lot of what was being said before the translation came.

They were Humans. Aliens. Friendly aliens, Sano emphasized. Not refugees from some attack.

(They learned later that the space station was on high alert as one of the nearby systems had been recently attacked by the Bukoykan.)

It took a few minutes of negotiating between the two computer systems before Sano was able to connect them visually.

A broad Lithic swam into view. Gray and black fur covered his snout and face, and his whiskers seemed extra-long. His ears, too, seemed larger and longer than the few Lithic Rosey had met. He wore what looked like a khaki outfit, some sort of civilian uniform, she assumed.

He gaped at them, his mouth open, showing a bright pink tongue.

"What kind of trick is this?" he thundered when he finally managed to come back to himself.

"No trick," Rosey assured him. "We are aliens. Different than the Bukoykan. And we are here to help."

"Help, huh?" he replied. A sly look came across his face.

Or at least that was how Rosey was reading his whiskers.

"Tell you what. I'm going to have you meet me on another ship, far from the station, in case this really is a trick. We can talk about your 'help' there," he said, cutting the line.

Rosey and Moe looked at each other and grinned.

"You're on," Rosey said.

"Good thing I'm up for the challenge," Moe replied.

The Lithic ship they met with reminded Rosey of *Aisha*. It wasn't top of the line, but it looked as though it had been lovingly maintained. Even though it wasn't that big, she assumed that it had hyperspace capabilities.

The interior hallway, once they stepped past the airlock, was a lot dimmer than the military ship they'd been on. Rosey wasn't certain why. She knew that the Lithic preferred less light than the Humans. Was the military just trying to keep their soldiers tuned up and on edge, ready to fight?

"Welcome!" boomed their host as they stepped forward. "I am Pukoow Lirsind, trader extraordinaire!"

Sano spoke to Rosey via her bonephone, the same way she'd

communicated with Dennis for years, so she was able to hear the Lithic and translate when needed.

"I am Rosey De Vries," she said, introducing herself first before the others. "We are Human."

There really had never been any question as to who was going to be leading their group. The Lithic were partially a matriarchal society. Pukoow had automatically addressed her first.

Plus, they hadn't bothered to disguise Sano's voice. The Lithic they met would be expecting a female who knew their language.

"You really are all aliens, aren't you?" Pukoow said, his eyebrows drawn together in what looked something like confusion.

"We are," Rosey assured him. "And we have met others of your kind."

"Really?" Pukoow said, seemingly astonished. "Who? When?" Then he shook his head. "Where are my manners? This is not the way to treat guests. My milk-mother would be dragging me off by the ear to give me a proper scolding. Please. Come with me, my very special guests! Come to my den."

He used that downward motion of his hand to indicate that they should follow him further into the ship.

He brought them to a small room that had fabric on the walls to hide the corners, so it felt cozy, though Dennis would have sneered at the brownness of it all. There were three small couches, also curved and not square, sitting close to a round table in the center. A tea service sat in the middle of it.

It looked to Rosey like something Moe would have used: a glass teapot with silver accents and matching glass teacups. It was all very beautiful.

Unfortunately, it smelled vile. Rosey would bet that it was similar to the tea that Wyrak drank.

"To new friends and business ventures!" Pukoow said as a toast after serving them all a cup.

Bracing herself, Rosey took a sip. It was just as bad as she remembered. She still managed to get down a swallow without gagging before putting the teacup in its pretty saucer back on the table.

"We've met several Lithic," Rosey said, starting the conversation off. "The two who traveled with us for a while are Wyrak 'Wrong Way' Hinga and Kooron Aliru. Do either of those names sound familiar?"

She knew that she was hoping for too much that either of them would be recognizable. Still, it was worth a try.

"No, I'm sorry, I don't know either of those two individuals. What packs are they a part of?" Pukoow asked.

"Wyrak was in the military, a pack navigator, third-class, for the Star Pack Fleet. His commander was Jiac Beowen," Rosey said. "We need to contact the Lithic military, to let them know where their wandering navigator has gotten to."

"I see," Pukoow said, seemingly deep in thought. "And you had someone else with you?"

"Kooron Aliru," Rosey said. "She's a merchant who escaped from one of the Bukoykan attacks."

"No one escapes from those," Pukoow said automatically. He shivered. "I've seen recordings of how the small ships destroy everything, leaving no survivors."

"You're correct," Rosey said. "But we arrived in time, just after the attack, and could save her after her lifepod had been shot."

Moe piped up. "She was at the *Mattus* space station when the attack occurred."

"I'd heard about that attack," Pukoow said. "I knew some of the traders who died. But you saved one?"

"We did," Rosey said. "And we'd like to save more. But we need to talk to your military about how our tactics will help them."

"Of course! Of course!" Pukoow said. He peered at them for a moment before he sighed and shook his head. "An automatic alarm went out as soon as aliens appeared in system," he assured them. "But who knows how long it will take for them to respond?"

"I'm sure that if you sent a second message, directly to Star Pack Fleet and commander Jiac, that they'd come right away. They would want news of their wayward navigator," Rosey assured him.

"Where is he now?" Pukoow asked. While for the most part, the trader seemed open and friendly, there was a caution to him as well. "Is he with you, back on your ship still?"

"No, he's making a presentation to one of the Human governments, to try to get you more aid," Rosey said, only slightly tinting the truth.

"This is all so exciting!" Pukoow told her. "To be pushed onto the intergalactic stage this way! My *mxalis* had warned of momentous occurrences this month, but nothing like this!"

"I'm sorry, what was that word?" Rosey had to ask.

It took a while for them to finally figure out that Pukoow was talking about his horoscope, as if the planets and stars nearby had some sort of influence on his everyday life.

It wasn't much better than hunting for Bigfoot as far as Rosey was concerned.

Still, that led into other talk, a mish-mash of words, with all of them contributing. Moe and Pukoow did start talking trade and goods, getting into fairly technical details about spoilage rates and methods of preservation.

They were just getting ready to go when Pukoow pulled out a slab that had been tucked in alongside of the couch he sprawled across. He typed one-handed for a few moments before sighing and shaking his head.

"All right, it's done," he announced. "I've sent word to the Star Pack Fleet and commander Jiac that they need to get their asses here quickly if they want word of their navigator." He sighed and shook his head. "My birth-mother would have had me prolong contact for another couple of days, to see if we could maybe develop a bargain first. However, if you really can help out in the war effort, I'm willing to give up my claim."

"We'll figure something out," Moe assured him. "Some way of doing business together."

That got him a smile, whiskers rising. "Aye," Pukoow said. "Though I must warn you, I'm no kit when it comes to the negotiation table. Guests are one thing. Business is something else."

"I would never assume that you were anything but a warrior, there," Moe assured him.

They said their goodbyes to the trader and headed back to *Aisha*.

Moe waxed lyrically about the business opportunities he foresaw.

Atilio seemed...thoughtful. Rosey knew that he wasn't a trader at heart, but a redneck tinkerer, like her.

They all went to their own separate cabins that night, to sleep deeply and let the future take care of itself.

Of course, the future was no polite host.

Sano got Rosey out of bed after nowhere near enough hours of sleep. Her screen showed the entire Lithic Star Pack fleet arranged around *Aisha*, a message on repeat demanding to talk with Wyrak.

"Tell them he's safe and we'll talk in an hour," Rosey instructed Sano.

She couldn't help but almost crack her face in two with her yawn.

Good thing Moe had a lot of coffee on hand. She suspected it was going to be a long day.

THIRTY-SIX

It didn't surprise Jun that Emperor Ogawa planned to meet Wyrak and Kooron in the formal throne room.

It did mean that she couldn't just slip in, unannounced. She didn't have time, though, to change into her full Princess regalia or put on her warpaint.

Hopefully her mother and other members of the court would forgive her for that.

Of course, Jamaal looked appropriate for just about anything. And though Harkeen was a bit underdressed, he still looked snazzy enough.

No, she was the one deliberately underdressed for the occasion, in clothes that were appropriate for an archaeological dig or a casual lunch, but not much else.

At least she had the appropriate passcodes and phrases to get her through most of the layers of security around the Emperor, though the prick from the bio-scan irritated her palm and made it itch, as always.

"You can't go in there, Princess Ogawa," the last guard said as they approached a side door that led to the throne room. (Jun knew that going through the main, front doors would be too difficult.) The guard was an older man who'd probably been in the employ of the Emperor for years.

Now that Jun thought about it, most of the guards she'd seen had been older, senior, and more trusted. That made sense, as they were entertaining aliens.

"Is it, or is it not, *my* governess that the Lithic—the aliens—have been using to communicate?" Jun demanded.

That just made the guard's face turn more stubborn. "That doesn't matter," he said.

"I order you to step aside," Jun insisted. "We need to get in here."

The guard shook his face. He opened his mouth as if to say something, then shut it again.

What? What did he want to say to her? Was there a way that they could be allowed in?

"Do I need to threaten him?" Jamaal asked, stepping closer and looming over the guard. "I could make him let us through."

"You could try," the guard smirked.

Before the situation could escalate, the guard held up his hand. "We can only allow a person access if a member of the royalty is in danger."

Jamaal moved so swiftly that Jun barely registered that he'd stepped forward, just that there were suddenly warm hands on her head and throat.

"Let us through or I'll break her neck before you can shoot me," Jamaal said.

His cold tone made Jun shiver.

The guard glanced at Jun.

"He won't hurt me," Jun mouthed, though given how Jamaal sounded, she wasn't completely certain.

The guard nodded. "In that case, I will allow you into the throne room. But you won't get that close to the Emperor."

Jun could barely nod her head as Jamaal was holding her so tightly.

The door opened. Harkeen went through first. Jamaal turned

them, so that Jun's body was between him and the guard, keeping that position until the door shut.

"My apologies, princess," Jamaal said, immediately releasing her.

Jun swallowed and rubbed her throat. She didn't think she'd have bruises there. She hoped.

"It got us through," she said, nodding to him and to Harkeen, then leading the way down the short hallway to the throne room itself.

The "day" room had large black pillars and was dimly lit, the only bright spot being Emperor Ogawa himself. The formal throne room was all white marble, with gold, green, and black accents. A huge throne standing on a dais took up the far end, made out of ornate gold with bright rubies done in a repeating pattern of lotus blossoms. The room itself wasn't that large. People weren't expected to stand there, but to flow in and out, walking past the throne.

A warning buzzer stopped Jun from stepping out of the hallway and into the throne room itself. She paused just before sizzling lasers sprang up.

One more step and they'd cut her to pieces.

Similar lasers appeared behind them.

"Who dares to approach the throne without a proper invitation?" Emperor Ogawa thundered.

A group of guards came running up, guns at the ready.

Jun gulped. The Emperor actually sounded angry.

"I am Princess Jun Ogawa," she stated. "I am here to help with the negotiations with the Lithic." Then she spoke in Lithic, greeting Wyrak and Kooron, asking how they were doing. She couldn't see them, as they were around a corner of the hallway. She did have a clear view of the Emperor, however.

Wyrak replied that they were both fine. Kooron asked if there was something she could do about this *tzlime* cage.

After Sano translated (though not the swear word), the Emperor appeared to reconsider.

"You have been accused of serious crimes by members of the Kollective," the Emperor warned. "Is that why you didn't accompany our guests into orbit?"

"No," Jun said immediately. "It wasn't safe for me to do so. My family has been threatened for some time now. You know about the unsuccessful poisoning of Prince Minato. I, too, have now been targeted."

"Is it safe for you to come forward now?" Emperor Ogawa said, seemingly intrigued.

"Not completely safe, no," Jun admitted. "But safer, and if we're successful, the danger will be gone shortly."

"I see," the Emperor said. He turned his head and nodded to someone Jun couldn't see.

The guards stepped back and the lasers disappeared.

Jun took a deep breath, straightened herself up, and became a Princess.

She sailed into the throne room as if she owned the place, as though Emperor Ogawa was sitting on the throne on her behalf.

She didn't have the clothes or the makeup, so she had to make sure that her *presence* was known. Jamaal may have softly sniggered, while Harkeen swore under his breath.

That just told her she was doing it right.

Jun made a formal bow to the Emperor, directing her comments to him while ignoring the rest of the court. Honestly, they didn't matter right now.

"Thank you for your indulgence, Emperor Ogawa," Jun said. "Let me tell you how we met our charming guests while someone gets them out of their containment enclosure."

Before any of the guards could object, she added, "You have not just my word but the blood of my entire family that you and all those around you are safe."

Jun knew that she was condemning everyone in her line to death if any harm did come to the Emperor from the Lithic.

Again, Emperor Ogawa looked to his right to a guard hidden behind a pillar and nodded.

From the noises behind her, Jun assumed that her request was being fulfilled. She told of Rosey examining an alien wreck (not going into any of the details about possible illegalities), finding the data chip, and the one word on the chip that pointed to the Atoylee—Bukoykan.

She admitted to finding the moonbase of the Atoylee and recovering all the papers from there, as well as *not* immediately telling the intergalactic community about the find. They were being chased, after all, and it wasn't safe. She may have possibly exaggerated the danger to her life at that point. (Then again, she may not have been, particularly since Itsuki was involved.)

"I do have those papers ready to be released to scholars," she assured the Emperor. Though she and Sano were planning on keeping the chemical compositions of the weapons under wraps. She could explain more about those to the Emperor when they were in a less formal setting.

Then she told about finding the second alien wreck, a Lithic war fleet showing up, as well as learning more about the Bukoykan.

"Brave Wyrak agreed to come with us," Jun said. "But we knew that wasn't enough evidence for the Empire to commit its vast resources to stopping a war. Particularly a war between two alien species. So we went searching for more evidence to bring to your august self. That was when we recorded an actual Bukoykan attack, and managed to rescue Kooron."

"These aliens, the Bukoykan, you call them, have started attacking Human worlds," Emperor Ogawa said, sounding displeased.

"Yes, I know. However, we couldn't have predicted that," Jun said. "We didn't know that you'd have the evidence you needed provided to you by them."

"How long have the Lithic been at war with the Bukoykan?" the emperor asked.

"Four years," Wyrak replied in passable Human common. Then he added in Lithic. "We won't survive another four."

"That we have had our first, true, live alien contact, here, in the Empire, pleases me," Emperor Ogawa said after a few moments. "That it has brought a war to our doorstep does not."

Jun waited, her breath stuttering. Surely Emperor Ogawa would do the right thing.

Jun—I have news, came the message from Sano. *Rosey and the others were successful.*

"We are not without weapons," Jun said, taking a risk and interrupting the Emperor while he was thinking. "The key to defeating the Bukoykan was found in papers left behind by the Atoylee. You should be receiving news of an attack that was recently thwarted."

That drew a gasp from Wyrak.

Jun wanted to turn around and smile at him, but knew that wouldn't be appropriate. Not yet.

"So we can approach this alien war from a position of strength?" the emperor asked.

"We can," Jun assured him.

Emperor Ogawa pierced Jun with a hard look. "You family has been loyal for generations. This opportunity will either raise you up, or curse your name for all eternity."

"I'm aware of that," Jun said, lifting her head proudly. "We will bring nothing but glory to the Empire."

Or at least that was what she hoped.

"Leave us," the Emperor said after a few more moments. "We must meet with our councilors, determine the correct course for the Empire."

"Thank you for your indulgence," Jun said with another formal bow. Then she turned and marched out of the throne room with Wyrak and Kooron directly behind her, followed by Jamaal and Harkeen.

Now, she needed just one last task taken care of.

Hopefully Emma would contact them soon, letting them know if the "distraction" worked or not, and if her family was finally safe.

EPILOGUES

EPILOGUE THE FIRST

It had surprised everyone how few of the Bukoykan Hive ships they'd needed to destroy before the insectoid species sought out negotiations.

Some had theorized that the Hive ships provided such a large part of their collective mind that even losing a few put them in jeopardy. Others speculated that the pain of losing those minds had driven them to the table.

Still others, not so kindly, suggested that bullies were only bullies when they were guaranteed a win, and turned into cowards when they weren't.

Moe didn't know what was true. He doubted that anyone could understand such an alien mind, not without becoming part of it.

Of course, there were stupid Humans proclaiming that everyone joining the Hive mind was the only way to guarantee peace in the galaxy.

Everyone but themselves, of course. They would continue on with their own separate identities, acting as shepherds to the rest of the gullible flock. Sounded too much like several other religions he knew.

Not that the Bukoykan would have them. Humans were too chaotic to join, even after so many genetic modifications as to make them no longer Human, unable to breed true with anyone else.

Despite all the noise, the Bukoykan, the Humans, and the Lithic had all managed a set of negotiations laying out their future terms.

The negotiations were nearly finished. Moe had been on the periphery of them, meeting with some of the Bukoykan and trying to establish trade.

So Moe found himself on the Bukoykan ship where the negotiations were taking place.

Normally, he didn't consider himself claustrophobic.

However, his head nearly brushed the ceiling here, he couldn't stretch out his arms without touching walls, and the lighting made him feel as though his eyes were straining all the time.

Everything curved as well. No straight lines that came from manufacturing. The ship was partially grown, which gave the walls a skin-like texture that Moe hated brushing up against.

He didn't even want to think about the smell, how dry and musty the air was, how it was both too hot as well as too cold at the same time.

Though he considered himself a passable trader, he and the other negotiators had run into an impasse when it came down to goods that the Humans and Lithic could provide to the Hive.

The Bukoykan had no need for luxuries. Everyone's mind connected to the Hive had a natural contentment and a lack of want for more. (The drugged-out stares of the few of the other races who'd joined in negotiations had led to some serious nightmares for Moe.) Famine was unheard of—the Hive mind accurately predicted shortcomings and worked to overcome them.

However, sweets, treats, and entertainment were also unknown.

Their empire didn't run on commerce, but on peace, contentment, and a single collected mind.

Why, then, were they so warlike when they met other species?

Everyone had their own theory. Moe's private speculation was that the Bukoykan didn't consider any being outside of the Hive mind to truly be a person.

Moe walked past Bukoykan guards with their shiny, blue, compound eyes and impossible-to-read bug-like faces. The four upper arms held rather large guns across their chests, with bandoleers of ammunition draped over their skinny shoulders. Their legs were rather stout and their knees bent backwards.

The leaders that Moe and the others talked with tended to have golden eyes, bulbous heads, and smaller mandibles. Much of their language was out of the hearing range of the Lithic and the Humans. Sano and the others had had their work cut out for them, trying to come up with a translation machine that all three races could use.

The Lithic still didn't trust the thinking machines that the Humans used. However, they were extremely grateful for the help when it came to destroying the Bukoykan ships. (Though they'd been asked, the Bukoykan didn't know why they'd withdrawn from the area near the Atoylee. They did have stories of the Great Sundering, but their memories from that time were vague.)

The Bukoykan were contained. For now. Lines had been drawn and agreed to.

Reparations had been settled. Everyone left that table unhappy, which honestly? Moe considered to be the best outcome, particularly since the only thing the Bukoykan had that anyone needed was raw materials.

Which was why he was there that day, to see if maybe they could figure out some additional trade agreements. Something that didn't involve the Bukoykan stripping yet another of their planets to provide the affected governments with more resources, but that might bring joy to their collective peoples.

Moe walked into the room the ship had set aside for all of them. The lights in here were slightly brighter, though the space was just as crowded. Kikio, the Lithic representative, was already there, standing to one side. She had orange fur with black spots, though the hair around her muzzle was a golden color, a sign of aging he'd been told. She'd been chosen by the Lithic government to be their trade representative.

"I greet you," she said, nodding at Moe.

"And I greet you," he said in response, both of them in Lithic.

Almost immediately, the Bukoykan representative joined them. They were much shorter, barely coming up to Moe's chest. Their golden eyes glistened, as if they'd just been washed. Though the front of their body was bare, showing their segmented front, a black cloak hung from their shoulders, covering the back of their carapace.

Moe knew that the clothes were a nod to them, to enable the nose-poor Humans and Lithic the ability to distinguish between the Hive representatives. Otherwise, the Bukoykan didn't bother with clothing.

This one had also adopted the name "Three" for them to use.

"Have you thought/considered our trade suggestions?" Three asked, because there was never any greeting given to another. They always got directly to the matter.

So much for social niceties.

Moe sometimes wondered if Sano might make a better negotiator than him.

"We have," Moe said. "The reeds you provided give no nutritional sustenance for us, nor will they provide a base for clothes or liquor."

"They won't make a good tea, either," Kikio added.

"Then we have nothing left to give you," Three announced.

"I have one additional item that I'd like for you to consider," Moe said, reaching into his bag and bringing out a small sealed jar containing a golden viscous liquid.

"This has passed screening?" Three inquired, seemingly intrigued by the color.

Again, no one knew exactly what the Bukoykan saw. But the tilting of the head to one side was a good sign.

"It has," Moe said. He twisted off the lid and held it out to Three. "It's food," he added.

A disturbingly long tongue unfurled from Three's mouth, dipping into the jar.

Three suddenly stood completely still. Moe had heard the description of what happened when the individual was occupied with the rest of the Hive mind but had never seen it himself.

It was like the being in front of him had turned into a statue. No one was home. Though he generally couldn't see life in those bulbous, compound eyes, now they seemed completely blind.

After just a few moments, Three shook their head minutely and said, "What is this? It is tasty/nutritious!"

Moe had *never* seen any of the Bukoykan react with emotion before this.

"We call it honey," he said. "Only a few species of bees make it. And only on Human planets." He'd checked with the Lithic, just to make sure. As they'd evolved from predators, they'd never developed the taste for sweets that the Humans had. So while they might have honey bees on their planets, they'd never created an industry around them.

"We know bees," Three said. "They make a substance that we cannot utilize."

"Our bees are different," Moe said gently.

"We will trade you for this," Three said, hefting the jar up and holding it toward Moe.

It took Moe a moment to realize that Three was asking for the lid. Moe closed the jar and it quickly disappeared into some cavity inside the person's carapace.

Was that to become their own private stash? Probably not, given the nature of their species. However, would they physically share it? Or was Three now the only one who would ever actually taste it, while everyone else just had echoes of the experience?

Moe nearly snickered to himself when he considered that perhaps he'd just introduced the concept of greed to the Bukoykan. Something valued by an individual and not shared.

"What type of landscape/terrain do bees that make honey need?" Three asked.

"It isn't just the terrain," Moe assured them. "It's an entire ecosystem that would need to be established."

"Yes," Three said. "We understand." They didn't sigh out loud, but the way their shoulders moved up and down reminded Moe of that.

Besides, the Humans weren't about to give up their monopoly on honey. Not if it turned out to be an actual useful trade good.

"Then we will have to trade for honey at first," they said. "Gold for gold, yes?"

Moe couldn't help but start in surprise.

Had Three just made a *joke*? A light-hearted comment that was almost social?

Not only that, Three jolted with surprise when Moe casually mentioned that there were many different flavors of honey, depending on the plants that the bees pollinated.

"Oh! We must taste/experience all of them!" Three exclaimed. "It is truly from the Maker/Creator!"

The relatively easy-going Three remained through the end of their negotiations before bidding them a good journey and leaving the room.

"What was that?" Kikio asked, just as surprised as Moe had been.

Moe shrugged. "A drunken Bukoykan?" he hazarded.

That earned him a snort.

"We will also have to negotiate about honey and bees," Kikio assured him.

"We'd be happy to," Moe said.

He left the Bukoykan ship bolstered by his success.

Not only was his little shipping company going to initially provide most of the trade goods that the Lithic needed, now it appeared that he was going to have an exclusive contract with the Bukoykan as well.

His star was rising.

Maybe high enough to be eligible for a certain princess to officially be interested...

To finally become *that guy*.

SECOND EPILOGUE

Duri didn't feel as though she wanted to pinch herself or anything stupid like that. Yes, she might be living the dream that she'd had ever since she was a little girl.

However, she was fully awake and *actively* directing her future. Not asleep and passively watching it unfold.

This was why she was on the Kollective Defender that was part of the Human negotiation team with the Bukoykan and the Lithic. Even though she wasn't in a cabin on her own but in a suite that she had to share with her assistant.

However, she'd *known* that there had been two different alien species. Stupid generals hadn't really paid attention to her. Seemed that she had made some enemies when she'd initially reported to them, so they'd gone off and done their own thing, then been caught with their pants down.

They should have listened to her.

It was only due to *her* work that the Kollective was here in the first place, negotiating with actual living aliens, because she'd been listening and watching and *planning* for all these years.

The latest news dispatch from New Rome had come through that morning while Duri had been sipping her tea in her suite.

The room looked like a prison, with gray upon gray. She hadn't thought to bring anything to liven the place up.

Maybe next time.

Still, she read the news with some pleasure. Seemed that some scholar, Kipling Viteri, was being accused of treason for leaking certain information about the Atoylee moonbase before it was to be announced.

Shame, that. Pity, really. The news article did mention that the matter was still being reviewed. Duri would admit that her hatchet job hadn't been as neat as she would have liked, as it had been rushed.

However, even if he was eventually proven innocent, he'd have a very difficult time finding employment. No one would trust him.

And that was really what mattered in the long run, wasn't it?

He should have known better than to cross her.

Before she'd finished her tea the door sounded. Someone was there to see her.

General Carrick.

It was probably too much to hope that the generals had finally come to see the error of their way. Still, she was pleasant and stood when the general came in, even going so far as to ask him if he'd like some tea.

She felt a chill along her spine when not only did he decline, he also refused to sit but stayed standing in the middle of the room.

"You have been busy," the general said without preamble.

He was dressed in a formal uniform, all those snazzy medals decorating his left breast. He wasn't quite standing at attention, but he was still ramrod straight.

"That is correct," Duri said with pride. "You know that I work tirelessly for the good of the Kollective."

What did the old bastard want? Or was he here to try to snatch away all the acclaim that by rights should be hers?

"Tirelessly? Perhaps. Carelessly? Absolutely," the general scolded.

The cold spread, freezing Duri in place.

He waved a hand. The lights in the room abruptly blinked.

Duri narrowed her eyes. She was aware that meant that no one was currently recording them. Whatever listening devices in the nearby vicinity had been temporarily disabled.

She didn't have that power, and was a little surprised that the general did. Then again, she was aboard a warship.

"What are you talking about?" Duri said, proud of how dismissive she sounded and acting as though she wasn't fully shaken.

"Rosey De Vries," General Carrick said. "That clumsy attack on her, on the space station *Lorenzo*."

"I was only doing your bidding," Duri said, spitting the words out at the general. "You asked me to take care of things. So I did."

"Not very effectively," the general said dryly. "She's now beyond everyone's reach. No one is to touch her. No one."

"Message received," Duri said with a nod. There were only a few steps left in her plans to discredit the racer.

Maybe after all this fervor died down, she'd enact them anyway.

"Then there's Scholar Viteri," General Carrick continued.

"He released information about Project Red Elevator before we approved it," Duri said, fighting back.

The general shrugged. "That has yet to be proven. Plus, you didn't read the room."

"What?" Duri said. What in the names of all the Hells was he talking about?

"Did you not realize that the Prime Speaker for the General Assembly is married to his daughter?" General Carrick thundered at her.

Duri blinked. How could she have missed that piece of information? Had it been buried? She'd have to investigate how that had happened.

"You have not only made me look bad, by association, but brought disgrace to the Kollective," the general continued. With another wave of his hand, the lights blinked a second time.

They were live again, for whatever audience the general had in mind.

"Therefore, I relieve you of your duties as Inspector of the Search for Live Contact," he continued, as if there had never been a pause in the script. "Your department has been defunded. The contact with the aliens has proven fruitful, but the Kollective now needs to focus on the aliens we *have* found, not searching for more. Thank you for your service. You need to come with me, now."

"But...wait!" Duri said. "My department's gone?" Her life's work, erased by a single stroke of a pen?

"Yes, to build the way for the new Alien Trade department," the general said, seemingly pleased with himself. "Would you like to meet the Inspector?"

Duri nodded numbly.

"You can come out now," the general said, raising his voice slightly.

Kiley, her assistant, came walking into the room.

"What? How?" Duri demanded.

Kiley gave her a serene smile. "I've been keeping track of you for a while, now," she said simply.

Duri had no words.

She'd been betrayed.

And here she'd gone to the effort of learning the woman's *name* and even offering her a bonus that one time.

Duri felt so stupid. Was that how the information about Kipling's relationship to the General Assembly had been missed? Had Kiley actively hidden it?

"You will come with me, now," the general said, reaching out a hand to Duri.

"Where?" Duri said, though she wasn't stupid enough to not

do as he'd asked. She would *not* make a scene and have to be carried, kicking and screaming, from her suite.

"You'll be comfortable enough down below," General Carrick assured her. "But you'll no longer have access to the upper decks, as you are no longer a member of the Kollective government."

Duri shivered at the absolute finality in his voice. She wasn't going to prison or being put in the brig. However, she was absolutely being shown her place, down with the enlisted and civilians not associated with the current negotiations.

She still held her head high as she left her suite.

Sure, she might no longer have her cushy office or job. She might no longer even be part of the Kollective. It would probably take her years to rebuild her powerbase, as she was going to have to start from scratch with practically no resources.

But once she did...they would all have to beware.

She'd make sure of it.

She could come back.

No matter the cost.

FINAL EPILOGUES

Ronald "Ajax" Jackson tried not to sigh too loudly when *another* fucking spreadshit arrived in his inbox.

Of course, his father addressed it to "Ronny" instead of "Ajax."

Then again, though Ajax still thought of himself that way, he understood that his pirating days were over, at least for the present.

The Allied Worlds' government may not have a lot of complicated laws in terms of how it governed its planets and its populations. People, for the most part, were allowed to do as they wished.

However, the sort of mind control games that Constantine had been playing were strictly illegal, even in the Allied Worlds. No slavery was allowed in any of Human space, and what Constantine had been doing skirted far too close to that line.

Plus, there was the whole hiding the information about the aliens attacking planets.

Constantine could have been a hero. He tried to spin it that way, that he'd been building a second fleet to protect the Allied Worlds.

Fortunately, no one bought into his bullshit.

He had bought enough politicians along the way to avoid being shoved naked out of an airlock. (Unconscious, of course. They weren't barbarians.) However, Ajax wasn't convinced that the twelve-by-twelve concrete box that the former warlord now lived in was any better.

Ajax did have to remind himself frequently that he was much better off than Constantine, though it might not feel that way sometimes.

His family had taken him back into custody, paying all the fines the courts had piled on him. Even though he blamed a lot of what had happened on the brainwashing, he still was planet-bound, unable to return to space until he worked off his debt to his family.

Which, according to his calculations, was only ninety years or so in the future. Compound interest was a bitch.

Was it worth biding his time? Not seeing the stars again, as they were meant to be seen?

Was it worth waiting until he was *old* before he could regain his proper place as a pirate? If he'd even live that long?

Possibly.

In the meanwhile, he'd work diligently for his family's firms. Show them how much he could accomplish, even if he was considered the *littlest pirate*. (Somehow, someday, he was going to get even with Rosey for sharing that nickname with his family.)

Even if it meant wasting his talents and sweating blood over the latest spreadshits.

Jun waited in Moe's cabin on *Aisha*, sitting on the bed beside the sleeping man.

Well, technically unconscious. That was a temporary thing, though.

She did breathing exercises as she waited, trying to keep her anxiety tuned down to a minimum. This *had* to work. It was kind of the ultimate test, after all.

And perhaps some level of fair play.

Eventually, Moe stirred. He briefly tensed, then relaxed utterly. After a few blinks, he managed to open his eyes.

Jun handed him the waiting water bottle.

Moe didn't bother coming fully up to seated until after he'd slugged down at least half of the water.

The grin he gave her simultaneously soothed her anxiety as well as made her heart race faster.

"Guess it was my turn, eh?" he said.

"You did give me leave to drug you whenever I felt it was appropriate," Jun pointed out. "You were the one who said that turnabout was fair play."

Moe gave her a deep chuckle. "So I did. But I will also say that I woke up to a *much* better view than you had, and hopefully less dire circumstances." He paused, then swallowed. "Again, I want to apologize for ever doing that to you. It was a horrible thing and you have every right to distrust me forever." He paused again, then said in a broken whisper, "But I hope you don't."

Jun nodded. Drugging Moe to unconsciousness hadn't necessarily felt right, though he had given his permission for her to do it. He just hadn't picked the timing.

"You've learned your lesson, now, right?" Jun demanded, possibly slipping slightly into Princess mode.

"I have," Moe said solemnly nodding. "I'll never drug you again."

"Good," Jun said. "As a Peer of the Empire, you should be much too busy to indulge in something so foolish anyway."

Though Moe didn't blush, or it couldn't really be seen given his dark skin, she still caught what appeared to be his eternal embarrassment at the rank that Emperor Ogawa had bestowed upon him.

However, it gave him a position in the court. Not as high as a member of one of the royal families. He didn't have direct access to the Emperor either, able to bend his ear privately concerning trade matters with the aliens. (The ones he reported to could do that, based on his recommendations.)

And her father had decided that he liked Moe, giving his permission for the courtship.

"Yes, Princess Jun," Moe said, doing as much of a bow as he could from his seated position. Though he came right back up again with a pained expression on his face.

Probably the remains of the drug in his system. Bending over even a little had made his head pound.

"Drink some more water," Jun instructed, touching his hand that held the water bottle.

Moe obeyed.

"We have a big day ahead of us," Jun told him. "First, we have a meeting with another Lithic trading organization—this one headed by someone named Pukoow Lirsind. Claims to be a friend of yours."

That earned her a grin.

"Yeah, we met him when we first entered Lithic space. Old horse thief," Moe said, chuckling.

"Yes, I remember the name, now," Jun said. This should be fun.

"Then we have to meet about honey production, this time with merchants from the Kollective," Jun said. She shook her head. "I still can't believe that you found a substance that makes the Bukoykan *drunk*."

Moe smiled sheepishly at that. "It started off as something of joke," he warned.

"I get it," Jun said. And she did.

Possibly it had been the thing that the Bukoykan needed to turn them from being aggressive assholes into, well, not exactly friendly, but much less aggressive assholes.

"Then, we have the most important meeting," Jun warned.

Moe raised his eyebrows, waiting for her to drop the boom on him.

"It appears that *someone* needs to start picking up the slack on this whole courtship thing," Jun informed him, feeling her own cheeks grow warm. "There needs to be an official announcement," she warned. "Pictures taken. Events attended, so that there can be public sightings of the happy couple. An entire schedule that needs to be set up."

Moe opened and closed his mouth a few times without words, doing a passible imitation of a goldfish. "Got it," he finally said, nodding.

He drained his water bottle, sat back on the bed, glanced at her, then slowly opened his arms.

"I thought you'd never ask," Jun said as she happily flowed into the warmth of his embrace.

There may have been a little smooching. And some serious snuggles. They'd have to work their way up to more.

It wasn't really important, though.

Moe had held her heart since the day she'd met him.

Finally, he was free to give her his own in return.

Wyrak tugged again at the collar of the civilian suit he wore.

"Would you stop fussing?" Kooron hissed from beside him.

"But it itches!" he complained. Again.

With a sigh, Kooron stepped in front of him and adjusted it for him. "There, is that better?"

"Uhm, yes," he said. And it actually was.

Wyrak still felt slightly uncomfortable being out of uniform. He'd been officially retired, though. His skills as pack navigator, third-class, were no longer the only thing he had to offer the Pack.

He'd been promoted to ambassador, which had its own internal ranking structures. He'd considered it a lateral transfer at best, so while he hadn't gained any rank, he hadn't lost any either. Giving presentations to the Council shouldn't have been in his job description, but the collected leaders always seemed to want to hear from him directly.

Fortunately, he wasn't alone. Kooron was part of his team. As she'd been a merchant, she had a much better idea of how trade worked. Whereas Wyrak understood Humans. At least as far as it was possible to understand the furless. Who were just so weird sometimes.

It took him a few seconds to realize that Kooron was still standing in front of him.

"Hey. Wrong-Way. You flying in the right direction?" she asked, smirking.

Wyrak took a deep breath in, smelling the familiar scents of nearby packmates. As well as the now constant smell of Kooron, who was still grinning at him.

"I am," he said as his soul settled.

Though he was still afraid that he was going to get smacked, he reached out for Kooron's hand and gave it a gentle squeeze. "Thank you," he said.

That got him a softer smile as she squeezed back, before releasing his hand and coming to stand beside him again.

He wasn't alone. He had to remember that.

There may have been some celebratory cuddles when the announcement came that the war was over. And possibly a bit of more intimate grooming between him and Kooron (though she'd initiated everything, as was right and proper).

Some day, she might even allow him to become an official part of her family pack.

In the meanwhile, the doors to the assembled leaders were opening. It was time for Wyrak to make his latest report.

With Kooron by his side, he was sure to always be flying the right way.

Jamaal was tending his plants in his aquaponics room when Harkeen came home. "In here!" he called.

Harkeen came and leaned against the door jam, casually giving Jamaal a once-over that caused his heart to beat a little faster.

Since coming back to *Lorenzo* things moved quickly between them. Jamaal had lost the lease on his place (due to some questionable property deal that the accounting department for the space station was still looking into) and there wasn't any way for him to get it back. Instead, he and Harkeen had applied for rooms together, as that was a much easier way to get a larger space. Plus, the new location was closer to Rosey's workshop.

As a recognized member of the Human team that had initiated First Contact, there had been a *lot* of credits attached to the prize. Though the group had split it, he'd had more than enough to rebuild his life.

This time, not by himself but with Harkeen.

"How are the plants?" Harkeen asked, not stepping into Jamaal's domain.

That was just one of the many things that Jamaal loved about the man, how respectful he was of Jamaal's space, while at the same time, more than willing to share everything of his own.

Jamaal would get there, to the same spot. Eventually.

"They're doing good," Jamaal said. He had a few seedlings that had gotten big enough to transplant, while he'd bought the rest of his current collection as ready-to-grow plants. "The fish are happy too."

He'd gotten an assortment of fish for the large pool, including shrimp, yellow perch, and a hybrid tilapia that had more flavor and could be kept better with other fish. It would be more than a year before he could start harvesting them. Still, he was looking forward to when that time came.

After Jamaal finished up with his chores, he came to stand in front of Harkeen. His lover still leaned casually against the doorframe with a soft smile, though he reached out a hand that Jamaal gladly took, welcoming his lover's warmth as always.

Harkeen looked good. He always did. Jamaal suspected that Harkeen would age gracefully as well. Maybe there would be a touch of gray at his temples to make him look even more distinguished.

"Whatcha got planned for the rest of the afternoon?" Harkeen asked.

"Not much," Jamaal said, playing the same, slow game. "Whatcha got in mind?"

"Depends. Whatcha got on under that robe?"

Jamaal took a quick breath in, then found himself looking at the floor. "Chest plate," he admitted.

"Hey, hey!" Harkeen said, reaching out with his other hand and drawing Jamaal's face back up so that he'd see the understanding in Harkeen's eyes. "It's okay," his lover said softly. "You don't have to go without your armor for me. You need to be comfortable with who you are. Don't rush it, don't try to be other than yourself. Not for me. Not ever."

Jamaal nodded, then pressed his face against Harkeen's palm when his hand shifted. "I am trying," he said softly.

"And I know that. And I appreciate it. Just not too far or too fast. Okay?" Harkeen said.

"All right," Jamaal said. He had at least worked his way down to just a chest plate from the short sharkskin armor he used to wear.

He just felt so naked and unprotected when he had *nothing* on under his robes. And not in a sexy way either.

"So just your chest is hidden, right?" Harkeen asked, his eyes going from concern to *smoldering*. "Other parts of your anatomy might be exposed? Easily accessed?"

"Possibly," Jamaal said with a grin. "You might have to check for yourself."

"I think I might have to," Harkeen said, taking a step backwards, drawing Jamaal with him. "Then, later tonight, there's an opening I want to attend," he continued as they walked toward their shared bedroom.

"Will there be dancing?" Jamaal had to ask.

Harkeen gave a sexy chuckle that sent tingles up and down Jamaal's spine. "Of course," he said. "If not in public, I'm sure we can find somewhere private to dance."

Jamaal nodded, happy that they were so in tune with each other.

As they entered the bedroom, Jamaal's comm beeped at him, announcing he had an important message.

Harkeen nodded when Jamaal silently asked permission, and he brought up the note.

Seemed that there was a possible new alien find to be explored, out on the edges of Lithic space.

Nothing Jamaal had to jump on right away.

No, while he might still be on the lookout for additional aliens, he'd found his prize.

Ironically, it had been right beside him all along.

Rosey sighed as yet *another* group of workers shlepped their way from the door of her abode on the space station *Lorenzo*, through her workshop, and onto *The Roadrunner*.

It hadn't taken long for her to be able to reclaim her space. First of all, the warlord Constantine had been so discredited, all of his legal contracts had been brought into question. Then, Ajax had been the one to actually sign the documents, and he was more than happy to waive any right he might have to her space.

However, even if he hadn't been, Erin Gratski—the station manager and a good friend of Rosey's—had added extra oversight clauses into the contract. She possibly could have rendered it null and void if Rosey had needed the help.

Rosey still felt a little bad about missing the deadline for the customer she'd had at the time, building them a speedship. Fortunately, she had an extra pair of hands in the workshop these days.

Atilio whistled in a breathy, out-of-tune way as he adjusted the timing on the engine he was working on. He still had his own space. And the pair of them, once they finished off Rosey's existing contracts, were going to take some time off from building speedships and instead, focus on making additional improvements to Human ships based on Lithic technology.

The main contracts had gone to a bigger company, of course. Rosey was a one-woman shop. She didn't want to scale up to that level.

She could, however, still be hired as a consultant. After all, she still needed to work for a living.

Everyone who'd been present when the Lithic had arrived had split the prize money for making first contact with live aliens.

Everyone except Dennis, who, for all his big personality, wasn't really accorded the same rights as a Human.

So Rosey had assigned her share to him, telling him that was his design budget from here on out so he had better not blow through it in the first year.

He'd whined, saying that the *Envoy to the Stars* and the *Savior of the Universe* deserved better. However, Rosey had stood firm.

Particularly when the assignation from the Empire had finally come through, granting *The Roadrunner* ambassadorial status. That meant that the Empire would also cover some of his design upgrades.

Plus, Rosey had found an accounting AI who wasn't "stupid," at least according to Dennis, who'd directed his funds into some interesting investment opportunities that had guaranteed that Dennis would now be set for eons.

So while Dennis hadn't touched the helm or Rosey's private quarters, he had updated practically everything else.

As soon as Rosey and Atilio had finished testing the prototypes for the new Lithic/Human engine designs, she would personally see to those being updated on *The Roadrunner* as well.

It was actually nice to have someone in the workshop. Atilio mostly stayed out of the way working on what she'd assigned him, happy to follow her lead. But an extra pair of hands sometimes came in handy when working on the more fiddly bits of this speedship.

Sure, she could always pull over the machine with the waldo-arms that Dennis could utilize. But Atilio seemed more in tune with whatever it was that Rosey needed, shifting around without being asked.

Just as they were finishing up for the night, Rosey got a message from Jamaal on her bonephone.

Seemed that there was another possible alien contact just waiting to be had at the edge of known Lithic space. Jamaal had received the message the night before, and had spent the day researching it.

And was Rosey interested in going to investigate?

Rosey couldn't help but roll her eyes. While Jamaal might have been credited for finding Humanity's first alien contact, he was still a Bigfoot hunter, still searching for yet more aliens.

She looked at the projects that were underway in her workshop.

If she could delay him just a day or so, then she'd have met her obligations, and could go on another screwball adventure.

That would hopefully turn out as well as this one had.

Atilio came over and Rosey asked him as casually as she could, "So, got any dinner plans?"

"Oh, I don't know," Atilio said with a grin as he wiped at the remains of the engine oil still staining his fingers. "What do you have in mind?"

"Jamaal might have a new 'lead,'" Rosey said.

"I see. Are they already on their way over here?" Atilio asked.

Rosey rechecked the message.

Crap.

"Yes," she said with a sigh. That man was going to drive her to distraction one of these days.

Then again, he knew that if she was elbows-deep in an engine, she might possibly forget to eat dinner. Again. As usual.

Coming over to "rescue" her as well as bring her dinner had been a pattern they'd developed over the years.

"They'll be here shortly," she added.

Atilio considered his hands for a moment longer. "Should we get cleaned up?" he asked cheekily.

"Yeah, I suppose," Rosey said.

That was the other really nice change: Atilio now had his own room on *The Roadrunner*. Sometimes he spent the night there. Sometimes he spent the night with her. They were both feeling their way through things, trying to find the perfect balance of togetherness and alone time.

Atilio paused for a moment, growing still.

"Race you!" he said, laughing as he turned and started jogging toward the airlock where *The Roadrunner* was connected.

"Cheater!" Rosey accused with a laugh as she raced after him.

Maybe she'd let him win. This time.

He could always make it up to her later.

Particularly after they'd figured out their next adventure with Jamaal.

ABOUT THE AUTHOR

Leah R Cutter writes page-turning fiction in exotic locations, such as a magical New Orleans, the ancient Orient, Hungary, the Oregon coast, rural Kentucky, Seattle, Minneapolis, and many others.

She writes literary, fantasy, mystery, science fiction, and horror fiction. Her short fiction has been published in magazines like *Alfred Hitchcock's Mystery Magazine* and *Talebones*, anthologies like Fiction River, and on the web. Her long fiction has been published both by New York publishers as well as small presses.

Find Leah's books on Knotted Road Press at (www.KnottedRoadPress.com)

Follow her blog at www.LeahCutter.com.

Reviews

It's true. Reviews help me sell more books. If you've enjoyed this story, please consider leaving a review of it on your favorite site.

Come someplace new...

Do you enjoy exploring strange new worlds, new cultures, new people?

Journey into the various lands envisioned by Leah R Cutter.

Sign up for my newsletter and I'll start you on your travels with a free copy of my book, *The Island Sampler*.

I will never spam you or use your email for nefarious purposes.
You can also unsubscribe at any time.

http://www.LeahCutter.com/newsletter/

ABOUT KNOTTED ROAD PRESS

Knotted Road Press publishes dynamic fiction set in exotic locations. Our authors cover a wide range of genres including science fiction, fantasy, mystery, literary, and poetry. We also have unique non-fiction voices in genres such as autobiography, business, cookbooks, and how-tos. We offer both DRM-free ebooks and print books for a global readership.

Knotted Road Press
www.KnottedRoadPress.com